I0520536

FORTITUDE'S PRIZE

Ceril N Domace

To my parents, my siblings, my friends, and everyone who supported me throughout my writing journey. Your support means the world to me as I branch off into a new world and series.

Copyright © 2023 Ceril N Domace

All rights reserved. This book or any portion thereof may not be reproduced or used in any manner whatsoever without the express written permission of the publisher, except for the use of brief quotations in a book review.

First Printing: 2023

Print ISBN: 978-1-7364301-8-7
Ebook ISBN: 978-1-7364301-9-4

Edited by Chih Wang of CYW Editing
Cover Design by Atlas Theseus Schmidt

For information about purchasing and permissions, contact Ceril N Domace at cerilndomace@gmail.com

www.cerilndomace.com

This is a work of fiction. Names, characters, places, and events are either the product of the author's imagination or are used fictitiously. Any resemblance to actual persons, living or dead, events, or locations is entirely coincidental.

Trigger Warnings: This books contains incidents of violence, kidnapping, piracy, false imprisonment, and piracy.

ALSO BY CERIL N DOMACE

The Fae Queen's Court
Haven
Avalon
Hiraeth
The Fae Queen's Court: Collected Edition

TABLE OF CONTENTS

Interlude 1

My first adventure on board the privateer *Vulturnus*, under Captain Mahaut Proulx, began when we were hired by the master of Fortitude Citadel to retrieve some of his stolen property. At the time, of course, we had no way of knowing what would come of this adventure, or perhaps Captain Proulx would've refused the letter of engagement despite the wishes of our engineers.

The master of Fortitude Citadel, which was the largest and most profitable of the fortresses in the Flying Isles, is a person of great and noble stature. In ordinary circumstances, he never would've stooped to hire a crew such as ours. The *Vulturnus* was a fine ship, but the master had numerous larger and faster ships in his fleet. I have been led to believe that our hiring was a matter of chance, the whims of the oracle bones, and the desires of a mourning sister.

In addition, the property that was stolen was of such worth that Master Thaddeus did not wish the theft to be widely known, and commissioning a vessel such as the *Vulturnus* would downplay the value of what had been taken. Knowing that the dangers associated with the voyage have now passed, readers would still be wise to remember that we had no way of knowing what would come of this adventure . . .

Chapter 1

The sun had long since begun its daily slide below the horizon when the *Vulturnus* made port on the flying island of Fortitude. The captain, Mahaut Proulx, and the quartermaster, the former scholar Hakim Kader, left the docks not long after nightfall. They sought ale, gossip, and work in the various taverns and places of ill repute under the protection of the master of Fortitude, Thaddeus the Black.

Most of the crew absconded to drink away their earnings from our previous commission—a rather boring trek escorting an unwilling merchant's son to the waiting bosom of his wealthy bride-to-be—and those of us left filled the dwindling hours of the day as best we could.

The first mate, an Englishman named Christopher "Kit" Duncan, decided to bring some levity to those who remained on the ship by teaching me how to wield a knife after the daily chores were completed but before sunset stole the light that we needed to practice safely. In ordinary circumstances, I was a fair hand with a knife. I knew how to whittle and how to prepare fish and game, but against the larger and more intelligent creatures that inhabited our world, I had few defenses.

Kit was a harsh taskmaster when it came to correcting what he considered deficits in my education, as were many of the crew. I eagerly capitulated to their instruction, since the man who had been my father had failed to teach me little more than the directions of the stars and how to stumble home after a long evening at the local pub.

Tonight's education took the form of attacking the quartermaster's mending mannequin. After each blow, Kit would correct my stance or adjust my arm. Occasionally, others among the crew would call out suggestions that Kit either took under consideration or returned with a vulgar gesture.

The lessons were a godsend, and I took both compliments and rebuke in equal pleasure. While I considered myself highly educated for the island of St. Bernard, not long after I joined the crew I found myself disabused of the idea that my knowledge meant much of anything on a ship like the *Vulturnus*.

My mother had seen fit to teach me reading, writing, and the alchemy that was her trade, but I lacked the innate magic my siblings and her or even my wretch of a father possessed. My own small talent in that regard was good for little more than breathing life into the most basic potions. My command of mathematics, if I am so bold, was considered superior to many that made the Flying Isles their home, and I was well studied in the art of local mercantile transactions, having handled the annual sales with my mother since I was small.

However, I could tie only the most basic of knots, my command of weathersight was barely superior to that of a mainland peasant, and—while my knowledge of the etiquette for dealing with the Liúwáng folk, who maintained the vessels that made the Flying Isles habitable, was second to none—my sailing knowledge was limited to the fishing boats from back home. The one griffin I'd known back home belonged to the innkeeper and was only good for chasing down rats.

Upon learning this, Quartermaster Hakim decided that I was a very intelligent young man much outside of my normal wanderings. He took it upon himself and the plethora of unique individuals that made up the crew to teach me the skills I lacked. Some nights, that meant eating in the captain's quarters, going over the navigational charts, and other nights, Alice spoke of the wonders of the heavens and the glories of weathersight while showing me how to feed the griffins.

And some nights, Kit pulled out the quartermaster's mannequin and his knives. These lessons I enjoyed more than all the others. Kit set up the training area in the middle of the deck, and any crew that wasn't on shift or on shore gathered around to teach me what they knew.

It was in the midst of these lessons—when Kit was explaining the virtues and vices of striking a man through or under his ribs—that Captain Proulx and Quartermaster Hakim found us. More specifically, it was when I finally managed to drive my knife deep into the mannequin that they strode up the gangplank.

"Mr. Duncan," Captain Proulx called, her voice thundering across the deck. "Are you done traumatizing my husband's tools?"

My heart leaped into my throat. I jumped back from the mannequin and spun to face the captain, whose frown could've cut a man in two. Quartermaster Hakim arched an eyebrow and crossed his bulging arms. On another man, that look would've heralded a fight. Right now, it mostly proffered disappointment.

There was a reason Kit usually waited until Hakim was out before he started these lessons.

Kit snorted and plucked the knife from my frozen fingers. "How else is the boy supposed to learn where to strike? On one of us?"

Hakim shook his head. "Of course not," he said, his voice a deep thrum that perfectly counterpointed his wife's sharp words, "but my mannequin is for clothes, not combat. Next time make a dummy from sackcloth and feathers."

Kit snorted again and bowed dramatically. "Of course, sir. I'm certain the griffins won't mind us raiding their nest."

Only a fool wouldn't have noticed the tension between Hakim and Captain Proulx as they strode toward us, Hakim a short step behind Captain Proulx. The other crewmembers scattered to the wind, the rigging, and below deck, where the echoes of Cook's dinner bell split the night.

Captain Proulx scowled as she walked. Her hair—long, twisted braids in the fashion of her African mother's people—and her long coat fluttered in the stiff wind that howled across the deck. Someone would need to speak with the harbor master tomorrow morning for the positioning. Who knew how far Fortitude would float tonight.

"Mr. Bardsley, tell Cook to bring three bowls to my quarters," Captain Proulx ordered, barely glancing at me while she examined the damage to the mannequin. "Mr. Duncan, help Hakim take the mannequin back to our quarters and then stick around. We need to discuss the commission we were offered tonight."

Hakim laughed and tucked the mannequin—weighted and unwieldy—under one arm without breaking step. "Nonsense, love, I can take it on my own."

"Your shoulder, dear—"

Snorting, Kit sheathed his knives. "I suspect we'll be needing Alice before the night is through." He glanced at me and jerked his head toward the door Captain Proulx and Hakim had disappeared through. "Captain gave you an order, Bardsley. Best get going."

Life returned to my feet as a blush flooded across my

cheeks. "Of course, sir. I'll get right on that."

"And if you see Alice, tell her the captain wants to speak with her."

I waved in acknowledgment and pulled open the latch to below deck.

The *Vulturnus* was not a large ship by the standards of the Liúwáng, but it was comfortable. The crew, a motley collection of folk from across the lands east of the Atlantic Ocean and natives of the Flying Isles, had no complaints at least. Captain Proulx and Hakim shared the captain's quarters on the opposite side of the ship. Our hold was smaller than most, as Kit lamented on many occasions, but he didn't complain that we had an ample galley, good food, and plenty of space to sleep or entertain a crew of over sixty souls when the weather was poor.

Hakim always said that a crew that was bored, hungry, or tense was worse for a captain than a hurricane. A happy crew kept the ship flying and the cargo in the right hands, and that was more important than a large hold.

The reason our hold was so small, of course, couldn't be helped.

Our engineers, who were Lin Yunru and his wife, Fan Ju, occupied a large, closed-off area at the back of the ship. It was there that they maintained whatever sorcery or science it was that gave the ship flight and there that none of the rest of the crew was allowed to go without explicit permission and supervision. The most I had ever seen of it was glimpses of red and the smell of unfamiliar spices floating out of their galley.

Their quarters were on the opposite side of the ship from the main galley, though, and that was my destination. Cook's dinner bell had already rung, and I had a mission.

Cook was a brawny Scotsman nearly a foot taller than me and six inches wider, and I wasn't a small man by any means. He told no one his given name and threatened to introduce his ladle to anyone who pushed the matter. Allegedly, after he'd been exiled from Scotland, he'd spiced and stewed his way across half of Europe and most of Africa. Fan Ju had even taught him a bit of Chinese cooking, according to the gossip I'd heard. I never found out if that was true, but I've never before had food prepared the way he made it, and I doubt I ever will again.

The chatter from the galley crept down the hall, Cook's thick burr rushing past it, accompanied by a chorus of laughter. Pushing the door open, I strode into the galley and was met with a wave of warmth and the scent of fresh bread.

My stomach gurgled and I swallowed instinctively.

Cook waved at me. "Welcome to dinner, Edward. I was about to send the dogs out for you. It's not like a lad your age to be late for dinner." He picked up a large roll with the center cut out, and spooned a heap of beef stew inside. "Lucky for you, I saved you some."

"Thanks, but I'm supposed to bring dinner to the captain's quarters. Three servings."

"Aye?" Cook raised an eyebrow and set the bread bowl he'd prepared for me aside. The chatter died down and many eyes fell on me. "Have we found a new commission, then? I was hoping to get a few days shoreside to restock my spices."

I shook my head. "Not yet, but the captain and Hakim wanted to talk to Kit about it."

"Hm. They want to talk to that bawbag?" he asked casually, laying four of the rolls on a tray and ripping the centers out. "Then they'll be wanting Alice too."

"That's what Kit said."

Cook snorted and shoved the tray with the rolls toward me. "I ought to have known. Here, she'll be in our quarters if she's here at all. Knock twice and she'll be out."

Kit, Cook, and Alice shared what ought to have been the quartermaster's cabin. They bunked together—Kit and Cook because they were arguably the most important members of the crew outside Captain Proulx and Hakim, and Alice because she scared everyone else and said she wanted some peace and quiet. How, exactly, she achieved that with Kit and Cook at each other's throats whenever news came of the latest English offenses in Scotland, was anyone's guess.

Nodding, I took up the tray and backed out of the galley. My stomach gurgled again, and Cook let out a sympathetic chuckle.

"Hurry back here when you're done, and you can have what's left."

Shouting back my thanks, I sped toward the captain's cabin. Thankfully, we'd already unloaded what little cargo had filled our hold on the way here, and Cook hadn't had time to restock his stores, so I didn't have to worry about tripping over anything. Some of the older sailors said they could navigate a packed hold with their eyes shut and both feet chained together, but I hadn't mastered that skill yet, and I didn't fancy trying when Captain Proulx, Hakim, and Kit were waiting for their food.

At least it wasn't far. I knocked on Alice's door twice as I passed, careful to balance the tray against my other hand and the door itself, and then rushed on.

I'd been in the captain's cabin a handful of times. Her tiny stateroom—which wasn't much bigger than the chicken coop back home, if I was being honest—was packed full of charts, maps, and various bits of paperwork Hakim kept threatening to burn if she didn't sort through it. In the center of the room, nailed to the floor, was a table large enough for four or five people to pack around, and it was there that Captain Proulx, Hakim, and Kit were seated when they called me to come in. It had been a miracle they'd heard my knock. Even through the thick wood I'd been able to hear raised voices.

"I'll take it from here," a soft voice whispered in my ear. Alice pushed past me in a wave of blond hair, the tray already in her hands, and Hakim nodded at me.

I blinked and awkwardly dropped my hands. The hold had been empty a short minute ago, and there wasn't a door on this ship that didn't squeal like a cat was caught in its hinges, but I hadn't heard her coming up behind me. By the isles, the others weren't kidding when they called her a ghost.

"Thank you, Edward," Hakim rumbled, passing the bread bowls around the table. He raised an eyebrow when Alice bypassed the open chairs and squeezed into Kit's chair instead, but didn't comment. "Tell Cook we'll need to speak with him in the morning, and then you can consider yourself dismissed for the night."

"Close the door behind you," Captain Proulx said, a knife's edge running along her words.

Wordlessly, I nodded. The steady thrum of their raised voices continued not even seconds after the door clicked shut, this time loud enough for me to make out a scant few words. Hakim's rumble was loudest, arguing about cost and distance.

I shook myself and took a step back before I heard more. "None of your business," I whispered under my breath. "You'll find out soon enough."

If there was one thing my father had been a stickler for before he'd succumbed to the drink, it was manners. He'd offended the wrong people once and regretted it for the rest of his life. I'd find out whatever I needed to know about our next commission when the others did, and I'd catch hell from Hakim if he caught me eavesdropping.

Besides, Cook had dinner waiting for me.

When I pushed the galley door open this time, there was much less noise. From above deck came the distant song of a mandolin and someone poorly accompanying on a fife. The night shift had started early today, taking advantage of a night in port to relax and enjoy themselves with the streetwalkers and passersby that roamed the docks.

"Did you find Alice?" Cook asked, setting a gently steaming bread bowl in front of me.

"She found me," I answered, giving in to the endless rumbling of my stomach and pulling my dinner toward me.

Cook laughed and dug into his own meal, to which he'd added a foul-smelling cheese and a bright red spice. "The lass will do that. No doubt she heard you knock and decided to have a bit of fun."

Shrugging, I swallowed a bite and then pulled out my canteen. The water inside was tepid and stale from hours at my side, but I wasn't brave enough to chance the poison that came from Cook's private still.

"You didn't hear anything?" Cook asked, pulling a flask from deep within his battered leather coat. He took a swig and then dumped a liberal amount in his stew. "Hakim normally stops by to let me know who to visit tomorrow. I can't very well stock provisions without his approval."

"Alice went right in and then they sent me out," I said matter of-factly. Cook was a bigger gossip than any laundrywoman or bartender I'd ever met. He knew nearly as much about the goings-on on the *Vulturnus* as Alice did and without the threats she employed to get her way. "Hakim said he'll speak with you in the morning, but I didn't stick around to listen when dinner was waiting."

Cook let out a hearty chuckle. "A lad your age? It's a miracle the food got there at all. My brothers and I ate our parents out of house and home when we were in our twenties. I'd not have stuck around to listen either." He pointed at my bowl, which, I'm unashamed to say, I'd already scraped clean. If he'd waited a few seconds longer, I'd have already had the bowl halfway down my gullet. "Come on, I've got a bit more stew left, and you eating it saves me from throwing it out."

***

Cook had enough stew left for two more bowls, and I left the galley well satisfied. He'd done his best to weasel what information he could out of me, but considering that I'd already told him all I knew, there wasn't much left to tell.

I suspected that he was simply jealous of his bunkmates. A man like Cook liked to be well-informed, and to be the last to know must have rankled him horribly.

Despite the pleasant buzz in my ears of a well-enjoyed meal after a hard day's work, I wasn't ready for bed just yet. An accordion and someone's fiddle had joined the ruckus on deck, and I was more than happy to follow their call.

The players had sequestered themselves on the fore part of the deck. Four streetwalkers, dressed in the required bright red of their trade, swung and danced around with a few of the night watchmen. An open barrel sat next to the mandolin player, its fumes enough to make my head spin from across the deck, and the dancers dipped in as pleased them. They must've been indulging since before I'd sat down to eat, because their steps had a noticeable lurch to them.

A cool wind blew in off the water, upwind of the dancers, and I was only too grateful to sit on the stairs farthest from them. Pixies danced far above my head, their ethereal glow lighting up the rigging like starlight as one darted down to spin around my head, its softly glowing hands lightening my brown hair several shades as it tried to pull me into the dance. I waved it off with a smile and leaned back onto the stairs behind me. The players would never be known for their craft, but they could carry a tune, and listening to music was a wonderful way to end a long day.

Despite not leaving the ship yet, I was enjoying our stay in Fortitude thus far. The last island we'd visited had been tiny and nearly barren. Cook had cleaned out its market just trying to restock the larder. Fortitude was another creature altogether.

Fortitude was the biggest island in this part of the Atlantic Sky. Its markets were known throughout the civilized world, and one could find everything from spices to magic gems to artifacts of long-dead civilizations in its stalls. Its quarters were some of the oldest and most diverse since the islands had been settled. Even the Liúwáng maintained an enclave in the deepest part of the city, under the protection of the master of Fortitude Citadel himself.

According to the stories, Fortitude was the first island the old mage ships had landed on when humanity began exploring the sky and before they met the creatures that called the Flying Isles home. The master had been there even then, and he'd given them permission to land on his shores, provided they shared food, coin, and news with him. Rumors of his fires and the open bounty of his land had spread like wildfire. The nobility of the time had found it fashionable to maintain a house and small holdings on islands like this, but it wasn't until the Liúwáng arrived with their ships—ones that flew without a mage at the helm—that Fortitude had become the center for trade in this part of the world.

The merchants, tired of the heavy taxes lining the nobles' pockets, had come first. They'd struck deals with the Liúwáng for their ships and their engineers, and the sky finally became more than a playground for those wealthy enough to sponsor mages.

They'd built the legendary walls, added to the great keep that overlooked the town, and built their homes right up to the edge of the island, looking down over the ocean miles below.

My father had loved it. "A gem of surpassing beauty," he'd called it. Loath as I was to admit it, he was right. Thousands of fires burned in thousands of hearths, sending sparks that shone like living jewels high into the night, climbing the hills of the city all the way to the citadel. The cries of griffins settling in their nests and the calls of guards and gentlefolk returning from the late markets reached my ears even here. High above it all, Fortitude Citadel stared down like a gargoyle.

In the light of day, its white stone walls gleamed like diamonds. In times of trouble, it was said, the whole population could shelter in there. Its stores ran the width and breadth of the island, and the springs that kept the town alive and in the air found their roots deep beneath the citadel, where the master made his home.

When I was little, my father had spoken of bringing us here one day. My mother and my sisters at least. He'd promised to buy them the world in these stalls. If he'd been able to make up for his offense, to have his exile revoked and been able to sail once more . . .

The drink got him first. I'd given up on him long before then, but seeing the lands he'd always talked and dreamed about . . . I almost understood why he went the way he did.

Tiny pinpricks lit up a dozen windows, no larger than the pixies still playing among the rigging, and I wondered idly if the master kept his clerks late. The music stopped, and I emerged from my thoughts with a start. The streetwalkers had chosen their clients, and the others had departed. Even the pixies had wandered off.

The night had well and truly fallen, and I had duties to attend to in the morning. I slipped below deck and climbed into my hammock, the siren song of my dreams beckoning me to their depths with the anticipation of whatever commission awaited us.

Chapter 2

I got my wish to explore the markets, if not perhaps with all the freedom I might wish. When the morning bell rang, a grim-faced Kit pulled Cook aside and handed him a list. While I couldn't understand the Gaelic blasphemies that left Cook's mouth when he read it, they were effusive and enough to have Kit slapping Cook on the back of his head.

"Bardsley," Kit called as Cook rubbed where he'd been hit. "You're with Cook today."

"Yes, sir." I shoved the last of my bread and cheese into my mouth and chewed furiously. Excitement thrummed through my chest, and I fought to keep a smile off my face. Now was my chance to get into the city. Perhaps I'd have time to find a gift for Mother.

Cook let out a throaty laugh. "Am I supposed to take him with me to the Swoop, then? Mel will eat him alive, and that's only if that blasted cat doesn't try to kill him first."

Kit shrugged and tossed a thick coin purse at Cook, who caught it with one hand and squirreled it away into his sporran. "Hakim gave the order, not me. Besides, we'll need those reagents, and he actually knows what most of these are."

Cook snorted. "Fine, but you owe me a drink."

Kit rolled his eyes. "Somehow I always do. Now shove off before Captain Proulx thinks you're shirking." He turned away, already yelling for someone to help him check the rigging.

Cook looked me up and down and sighed. "Well, we

best be off. Be a good lad and go below deck for my satchels. We'll need at least three based on this list."

Nodding, I turned and ran below deck. A few weeks ago, I'd have been annoyed at how aggressive Cook was, but experience had taught me otherwise. Experience and Alice telling me off when she'd heard me grumbling about him one day. Apparently, he just didn't trust people to shop with him when he wasn't sure of their taste. When I proved I could tell when a merchant was trying to pull a fast one, he'd be more than happy to have me.

She'd also said that they'd had more than a few farm boys like me that weren't able to do that, so his aggression, in his eyes, was well-founded. There was a list hidden somewhere of crewmembers who weren't allowed on supply runs with Cook anymore. The fact that I'd made it through one supply run already spoke well of me.

Cook took off down the gangplank as soon as I emerged from below deck, and I followed at his heel. The docks were already packed, and it was barely an hour past sunrise. Despite the roiling excitement rushing through my stomach, I hardly dared look away from Cook's broad shoulders for fear of losing him in the crowd.

But the glances I risked were worth it.

Merchant vessels and privateers like us crowded around the dock, jostling for the rare opening to unload their goods and passengers. The stalls I'd glimpsed last night, closing down as the sun disappeared below the horizon, had opened again, and their keepers filled the air with their calls. Everything from jewelry and clothes to gunpowder and knives was available for perusal and purchase. If this was the dock, I wondered what was available deeper in the city, in the markets proper. One could find the world for sale here. My father hadn't been wrong on that account.

A fisherwoman's cry took my attention from the

merchants. Her nets brushed the top of Cook's head, chasing a rogue school of fish, and he released a storm of blasphemies in her direction. Her voice answered him in kind, cursing him for chasing the fish away, and then she took her ship higher still to avoid the chance a guard would catch her fishing for folk as well as food.

Hers wasn't the only vessel in the air. There were perhaps two dozen boats just like it wherever I turned to look. They chased cod, haddock, and mackerel between Fortitude and the unnamed islands that drifted around the edges of the water. None of those boats would manage far from the shore. The natural magic that gave them flight was bound to the island itself. St. Bernard, my home island, had many just like it. My mother always hated when my friends and I would go out on them.

"It's not safe," she'd say, elbow deep in reagents for whatever potion or commission a passing merchant or visiting farmer wanted from her. "If you go too far, you'll fall."

I hadn't taken her seriously then. Not, at least, until one of my friends had dared another to go farther than our parents allowed. We were very lucky that day.

That was the risk of flying without a Liúwáng ship or a well-trained mage. Fishing was not something for the faint of heart.

"Bloody fisherfolk," Cook muttered under his breath, "almost took my bleeding eye out."

He scoffed and then turned back to me, wearing a look that could've been concern. "You all right there, lad? They dinnae get you?"

"Oh," I said, scuffing my feet. I didn't want to admit I'd been so distracted by the fish that the fisherwoman could've hit me and I doubt I'd have noticed. "No, I'm fine."

"Good." His face fell into a familiar scowl. "I dinnae bring you with me only to see you brained by a half-wit with a net."

He didn't want to bring me at all, I wanted to point out. I held my tongue if only because I knew well the risks of angering the person responsible for feeding you. The last thing I wanted was to have to make something edible out of salted beef and hardtack because Cook had exiled me from the galley. I'd seen what happened to Kit the last time he and Cook got into it about the rebellion. It had been a month before he'd been allowed back into their cabin and two before Cook allowed Kit back into the galley.

Cook's muttering continued as we left the docks behind us and entered the city proper. Once he moved on from the fisherfolk, he ranted at great length about the quality of product available in the docks district and how one could hardly find decent spices at the waterfront. He answered all the questions I had long before I was able to ask them if only because he had an opinion about everything we passed.

I'd never been in a city quite like Fortitude. Once off the docks, the buildings closed in on us like storm clouds around the *Vulturnus*. Most buildings stretched three or four stories up and leaned on their neighbors like drunks. The lower levels in this district had stalls and shops with awnings to block out what little sun made it past the buildings themselves. The cobblestone was more compact and solid than any I'd ever seen—back home, only the market road had any sort of paving—but was littered with refuse, detritus, and worse. A month ago the smell alone would've made me vomit. If I hadn't spent the intervening time in close quarters with several folks who believed being asked to bathe was a personal insult, I might have done so anyway.

The oddest thing was how hard it was to see the sky.

I wasn't a mainlander. I'd spent my whole life in the flying islands, even if St. Bernard was isolated from the more populous of the isles. The sky was inescapable. Even in basements and cellars back home, we made very sure to stay aware of how much ground was between us and the open sky below the island. On ships like the *Vulturnus*, you respected the sky. It held the stars and the islands and the fish we fed on when rations got low. To see the sky meant knowing your way home and your place in the world. I couldn't see the sky here unless I looked up.

I took a deep breath through my mouth and resolved to stay close to Cook. If I lost sight of him, I wouldn't be able to find my way back to the ship. Bloody hell, what was the mainland like if Fortitude was this enclosed?

Cook's path took us to the market proper, and I'm not ashamed to admit I gasped like a schoolboy given a box of sweets.

The market thrived with life. Hundreds of stalls were packed into an area more than twice as big as the market back home. My nose was assaulted with dozens of spices and breads and meats hawked by merchants from all corners of the globe and reaches of the sky. Cook, wisely perhaps, took me by the arm and dragged me from one end of the market to the other, briefly stopping to haggle or to chat with merchants he was acquainted with. Try as I might to pay attention to the matter of business, my attention wandered, and Cook had to call my eyes back to the task at hand three times. As the satchels I'd brought gradually became weighed down with Cook's purchases, I was reduced to a beast of burden gawking at my surroundings while Cook spoke with the merchants.

A half dozen languages I recognized and more than a dozen I did not drifted across my ears as we went. French came from a stall selling fine New World furs, Japanese from a carpenter's stand, and some manner of fae language from a smith. African folk in bright colors with long, braided hair bartered jewelry and salt for spices and coin, Chinese merchants dressed in delicate silks argued over the quality of furs, a Dutch man loudly argued with an Indian woman in an ornate blue saree over the cost of her carvings—

It was everything I'd ever heard and more.

But all those wondrous things failed to hold my attention when the yelling started. My eyes left the merchant Cook was haggling with and traveled to a small guardhouse in the middle of the market. Well, yelling would be putting it lightly. It was a mix of howling and sobs with a constant flow of apologies mixed in. Either way, it was loud enough to draw the attention of half the market.

The source of that terrible noise was a man in chains, held on his knees by two muscular guards. In front of him was a person dressed in color-changing robes that leaked so much magical energy, even I could feel it. They held a small wand in one hand and drew up a whirling ball of light in the other, which they applied to the wand.

Its sickening glow turned my stomach when the chained man renewed his screams. A girl charged forward out of the crowd, adding her voice to the man's. Another guard grabbed her before she could make contact with him.

I unconsciously took a step back and swallowed. This was a branding. Whoever that man was, whatever he'd done was bad enough that he was going to be marked for the rest of his life so everyone around him would know his crimes.

But just in case any around would doubt it, three figures

in fine clothes stepped forward. The one in the middle, a short man in a fancy white wig, began speaking in clipped Dutch. My grasp of that language might have been only middling, but it was more than enough to understand what was being said. And, just in case I somehow didn't, the other two men repeated it in French and English, which I spoke fluently.

This man had been accused and convicted of assault and public intoxication. Over the course of a drunken evening, he'd gotten mixed up in a bar fight that saw six bystanders injured and one killed. While fleeing the premises, he'd injured a Liúwáng engineer. The sight of that had made the other participants turn on him, and they'd held him in place until the guards turned up.

He was to be exiled and branded so that all knew he wasn't to be trusted and wasn't allowed on Liúwáng vessels.

With that said, the girl let out a loud sob and screamed for the man, her father, while the mage stepped forward to do their duty. The man's whole body shook as the wand pressed into his cheek, and the magic painlessly seared into his flesh. When it lifted off, an E was inked on his flesh in bright green.

"Poor bastard," Cook muttered under his breath, tugging me in the other direction as the guards dropped the now-motionless man to the ground. "He'll never work again."

Swallowing harshly, I nodded and quickly looked away.

Exiling was an unfortunate necessity of life in the Flying Isles. The Liúwáng had their own method for marking exiles, one that only they could see, but they hadn't been the ones to decide to brand exiles so others could as well. That had been merchants too scared of losing access to Liúwáng engineers to risk hiring someone the Liúwáng refused to allow on their ships. Even if the Liúwáng forgave that man and revoked his exile, that brand would stay with him forever. No merchant would risk removing it and few would want one tainted by an exiled relative on their ship.

It was a hollow comfort to know that this was still a kinder process than it used to be. In decades past, criminals had been branded with hot iron to mark their crimes for all the world to see, but modern branding was little more than a magical tattoo. Just as permanent and just as prominent, but it had the benefit of being applied without causing further pain to the one exiled.

That was the only benefit. That man, like so many others who'd been exiled before him, was ruined, tainted by the mark on his cheek. People would avoid him and his family, refuse to pay fair prices for their goods, and their children would be passed over for opportunities as long as they stayed in the Flying Isles.

It was a horrible life. Most exiles returned to the mainland, where people cared less about the brand, and they might be able to eke out a living for them and their families on solid ground.

I shook myself and turned back to Cook, pushing those thoughts out of my mind and swallowing back the nausea. Lingering over them wouldn't help anyone, least of all myself. If I wanted to avoid a similar fate, I should pay attention to what was happening here and now, lest my inattention drew the focus of those I wanted to avoid.

After what felt like hours of wandering between stalls, Cook paid a pair of dark-skinned merchants in colorful robes for a pair of golden bracelets inlaid with turquoise, then declared we were nearly done. The sun shone fiercely down at us, unusually warm for this time of year.

"Just the Swoop now." He pocketed the bracelets and

scanned the market. His lips turned down in a sharp frown when he noted how crowded it had become. "Come on, it'll be faster this way."

Despite my aching legs, I followed, desperately hoping that whatever sort of store the Swoop was, it had a place to sit. Cook led me down an alley just off the main market, one hand buried in the pocket with the bracelets and the other resting casually on his dirk.

"What kind of place is the Swoop?" I asked when he paused to reorientate himself. My stomach growled loudly and I swallowed. My breakfast of bread and cheese had been hours ago, and the fading scents of the food in the market weren't helping things. Perhaps the Swoop was a tavern. Taverns had food and seating.

Cook flipped a small coin at a passing woman hawking potpies and snagged two from her cart. "It's a store." He shoved one of the pies at my chest, and I took it without thinking. "Here, lunch is on me. You're a good mule, if nothing else."

I bit into the pie and was greeted with a heady mix of beef, carrots, and onion. My stomach gurgled happily. "But what kind of store?" I asked through a mouthful of food, momentarily grateful my mother wasn't here to lecture me about my table manners. Cook's reaction earlier had me curious, I'll admit. He'd grumpily but willingly answered my questions while we were in the market, and even asked my opinion on a few prices. Now he barely seemed to want to talk at all.

"A pawnshop. Mel deals with misplaced enchanted items and information." He grunted and then viciously bit into his pie. "Bit of a berk, but their information is good."

"And you don't like them?"

Grunting, he pulled his flask from his pocket and took a swig. "The store's creepy. The employees more so."

I wanted to ask more, but nearly lost my pie when my boots caught a loose cobblestone, and I devoted myself to making sure that didn't happen again. By the time I licked the last of the crumbs from my fingers, we'd made it to our destination.

The Swoop occupied the ground floor of a run-down tenement closer to the docks than the market. A battered sign hanging above the door depicted a raven diving for a golden necklace, and that motif was repeated on the windows, which were so filthy that I couldn't see through them.

Cook wavered on the doorstep, one hand in his pocket and the other on his dirk. His face was set in a sharp frown like he was debating whether it was really necessary to go in or not.

"Cook?"

He sighed and stepped forward. "Come on. They're probably expecting us."

The hinges creaked when the door swung open. A large calico cat lying on the counter opposite the door raised her head to glare balefully at us for disturbing her nap. She let out a plaintive yowl before dropping back down to sleep.

"Yes, yes," said a voice from deeper in the shop. "I'll get around to fixing it eventually, there's no need to yell at me."

The inside of the Swoop was ten times more chaotic than the entirety of the market put together. *Things* were stacked everywhere. On one side of the main room, gilded furniture shared space with intricate clocks and open wardrobes spilling ornate clothing onto the floor. On the other, enough weapons to arm the entirety of the Fortitude guard hung off the walls and ceiling or was laid out on a table alongside a small changing area and a large crate overflowing with jewelry which had "cursed" written on all sides in a large and blocky hand. If I stood on my toes, I could see a door leading into a meticulously ordered library and another that led into what looked like an alchemist's shop.

The cat yowled again and then hissed.

"Well, is it anyone important?" the unseen speaker asked before there was a crash of falling cutlery.

The cat sneezed, stretched, and then let out a string of chatter as she shifted to her haunches.

"Customers? Well, why didn't you say so?"

The speaker emerged from the alchemist's shop, wiping their hands on one of the plethora of multicolored scarves that hung from their belts. From the top of their large bronze alchemist goggles to the bottom of their knee-high black leather boots with an improbable number of buckles, they were the strangest person I'd ever seen. Between the two extremes, they wore a heavily embroidered red coat and sturdy brown trousers, which were the plainest thing about them. Even their hair was a bright and unnatural blue, a stark contrast to Cook's black hair and my brown.

"Welcome to the Swoop," they exclaimed in a loud and forcefully friendly voice, "the finest purveyor of interest on this half of Fortitude! What can I do for you today?"

"Mel!" Cook exclaimed, holding his arms open wide. "I haven't seen you in ages. How've you been?"

Mel rolled their eyes and swatted at Cook. "Oh, it's just you. I wouldn't have hurried if I'd known that." They glared at the cat and huffed. "Come on back, I suppose you'll be wanting to speak with Konstantyn, then? You're never here to visit me."

"I'm wounded, Mel," Cook said with a convincingly affronted pout. "You know how much I cherish our visits."

I greatly doubted that. I'd seen how reluctant he was to enter the Swoop in the first place, but I knew a bargaining technique when I saw one. Mother used a similar method when dealing with some of the stupider merchants back home.

A meow and a tug at the bottom of my coat drew my attention away from Cook and Mel. The calico pawed at me again, and I leaned down to scratch her behind the ears. "Hello," I crooned. "Who're you?"

The calico purred and leaned into my hands. My fingers caught on the braided leather collar around her neck. A matching leather tag hanging from it had "Delilah" stamped on it in letters identical to those on the crate of jewelry.

"Afternoon, Mel!" The door swung open and slammed squarely into me, startling Delilah into sprinting behind a stack of apple crates. A plump woman decked out in furs and leathers strode in—a German if the thick accent coating each word was any indication—dragging a heavy-looking sack behind her. She either didn't notice or didn't care that she'd hit me, because she plopped her sack in front of Mel and smiled like a feral cat. "Got some good stuff for you this time. Where's Konstantyn?"

I stood, making a show of rubbing my arm and stretching. It hadn't hurt, but I'd still have appreciated an apology. Cook caught my eye and shook his head, exasperation briefly stealing his genial smile away. It restored itself before either of the other two could notice its absence.

"Elle, lovely to see you again," Mel said, smiling far wider than they had when they recognized Cook. "Pawning the profits of your raids, are we?"

"It's my legal share, I'll remind you. I'm a proper privateer these days," Elle said, turning her nose into the air. She nudged the sack with her foot, and metal banged against metal inside it. "Besides, I already traded off all the stuff that could be traced to my ship."

Mel nodded approvingly and picked the sack up with one hand. They then set it on the counter and immediately started rooting through it. "Good. I want no more problems with the master than I already have." They pulled out an ornate candlestick that gleamed with an inner green flame, then tossed it aside like it was garbage.

Cook coughed, and Mel shot him a baleful glare.

"Wait your turn."

"We were here first," I exclaimed before I could stop myself. My pride and my arm—to a small degree—had already been injured in this shop. Were they now going to ignore paying clients for selling ones?

Cook sighed. "Much as I hate to interrupt your tête-à-tête, the lad has a point, and I've a list." His smile took on a harried edge, and he proffered the scrap of parchment that held our list. He hadn't, for reasons unknown to me, actually let me see it yet. That was another thing Alice said he was touchy about, but I wasn't sure how he expected me to find the right reagents if I wasn't allowed to look at what Hakim thought we needed.

Mel let out a thunderous sigh and dropped the sack. "Fine. Elle will need to speak with Konstantyn anyway. He's got a better eye for judgment than I do." They came around the counter and plucked the list from Cook's hand. They read through it, muttering under their breath, too soft to hear, and then tossed the list back to Cook. "Come on. Elle, you too. Most of this'll be in the greenhouse."

Elle tugged her sack over her shoulder—making sure to grab the candlestick before she went—and followed Mel through the door to the alchemist's shop.

"Don't touch anything if you don't know what it is, and

27

touch even less if you do," Mel called over their shoulder. "I've got some delicate experiments going on back here, and the last thing I need is some dolt ruining it by adding wormstongue at the wrong time."

The workshop was incredibly ornate. Ten-foot-tall bookshelves lined three walls, each meticulously marked with the sort of books that could be found there. If we'd had more time, I'd have begged Mel to let me look through them. Even the faint glimpses I got hinted at titles and subjects my mother would've sold everything we owned to peek at.

Equipment in the form of beakers, burners, measurement tools that glowed with unholy light, and neat drawers of reagents were stacked high on tables pushed against the fourth wall. The reagents alone could've bought St. Bernard three times over with plenty left over to demolish the town and build it anew afterward, but I'd only ever seen sketches of most of this equipment. Even the enchanting circle on the far end was better suited for a mage's tower than a small shop.

That being said, the only thing even vaguely resembling an experiment that I could see was a glass teapot bubbling merrily over a blue-fire burner. The liquid inside shifted rapidly from green to red to black and then back to green again without pause. My mother's workshop—and the section she'd given to me when I completed my apprenticeship—had been packed with commissions and experiments in various stages of completion. When one was the only alchemist for hundreds of miles around, one always had more work than they could handle. Having a second pair of hands in myself and later my younger sister had been the only way she could keep up. Although, in a city the size of Fortitude, it appeared that Mel had more freedom to pursue their own interests. Especially if the

Swoop was profitable enough for them to just have most of these things lying around.

"Hurry up! That mix is particularly volatile. I don't want to have to explain to Captain Proulx why one of her crew was turned into cheese in the middle of my shop."

I jolted out of my trance and hurried after the others. Partially because I didn't want to get left behind, but mostly because I didn't want to think about why they were working on a potion to turn people to cheese. It wasn't the strangest experiment I'd ever heard of, but it was up there. Mother once told me of a man she knew who spent most of their acquaintance working to turn statuary to flesh and bone.

Mel rolled their eyes at me as I hurried through the far door, and closed it behind me. Our group now found ourselves in a long hallway with doors spaced evenly ten feet apart on both ends, each with their own label written in a now-familiar hand. The door across from the lab, which was labeled "office," had an extra sign hanging off the knob that read:

"Delilah, keep out. Tea cozies and ledger books are not for napping upon."

Someone, likely Delilah, had taken affront to this message and torn the lower half of the note almost entirely off.

Cook elbowed me in the side. "Some lab, eh, lad?" He smiled softly and followed Mel and Elle down the hall. Periodic snatches of conversation flowed back to us, but considering the few words I heard consisted of *explode, liquefy,* and *scrumptious,* I decided I didn't care to hear more. "The last alchemist we had damn near deserted just to have a chance at apprenticing under Mel. They're one of the best in the business."

I nodded and glanced backward to the lab. "I've never

seen some of that equipment outside of books. What's their specialty?"

I was a generalist myself, but I'd admit to leaning more toward the theoretical side of potions than my mother. She'd been focused on the practical applications of the things she taught me. Admittedly, those same lessons were why I now found myself off St. Bernard, but that didn't mean I wanted to spend the rest of my life brewing healing potions and mixing salves. Even if I didn't have much innate magic, I still wanted to make my mark on the alchemical world.

"Tea, from what I can gather." He jerked a thumb back toward the lab. "Never, and I mean never, accept their tea. Last time I did, I ended up purple for two weeks."

"That was the bluebells," Mel called over their shoulder. "Delilah thought you looked lovely in that shade, by the way."

"Aye, and the captain about laughed herself sick when she saw me," he shot back. "I'm saving the lad of trouble I went through."

Mel waved a hand around as if that would chase away Cook's accusations and came to a stop in front of a door made of glass and bronze wiring. The room beyond was lush with plant life in all colors of the rainbow and several that must have existed outside that spectrum. "No matter, we're here."

Greenhouse, as it turned out, was not the proper name for this room. While half the room was covered in plant life—everything from common garden herbs to alchemy reagents like Queen Ellis's root and something that glowed with a vivid purple light—the other half was a sitting room not so different from my mother's.

There were two or three bookshelves stacked with novels, an encyclopedia set that looked like it was mostly there for show, and dozens upon dozens of alchemy trade journals. Three overstuffed armchairs and a decadent couch were gathered around a low coffee table, upon which sat a steaming coffee pot and a handful of mugs that didn't match. In one of the armchairs was a large unfamiliar man with numerous tattoos, staring straight at me like he wished to devour my soul.

I stopped cold in my tracks. This man was a stranger to me, and yet his glare suggested I had done inappropriate things to his mother, sister, and father in that order after leaving him at the altar. He hadn't even blinked yet, and the others had already sat down.

"Come on, boy," Elle called, dropping her sack next to the man with a loud thud. She grabbed the largest mug and filled it nearly to the brim with coffee before taking it all the way there with cream and sugar. "Konstantyn only looks like he'll bite."

"He knows better than to bite now," Mel interjected, pulling a metal canister from within the endless scarves around their waist and glaring disdainfully at the coffee. "The last time he did it, they bit back."

Cook filled his own mug halfway full and topped it off with whisky. "It's all right, lad, he's just judging the look of you. It's what he does."

Keeping a careful eye on Konstantyn, I edged around the table and sat next to Cook on the sofa. The cushions beneath me were like a tiny feather bed, and I wondered how much it had cost Mel to buy them.

Konstantyn broke his silence—and his glare—with a grunt. He took his coffee black and leaned back in his armchair. "The boy will do," he said in a Russian accent so thick he might as well have been speaking in a different language. "Replace that waistcoat, though, it does nothing for him."

"What's wrong with my waistcoat?" I asked before I could think better of it, confusion having robbed my tongue of sense. "My younger brother made it for me."

Oliver had made most of my clothing, actually. Mother had enchanted a loom and spinning wheel to produce the cloth and dyed it the colors my brother wanted with leftover reagents. It took a lot of magical energy, but it was miles cheaper than paying through the nose for material from one of the villagers that looked down their noses at us and complained when Mother charged fair prices for her work. My brother might not have been the best tailor in St. Bernard, but he knew how to make the basics. The only thing he hadn't made was my leather work apron, which my mother had given me when I completed my apprenticeship.

"It's a poor showing, and your brother needs more practice. The stitches are coming out, and a blue color would suit you better than brown to match your eyes." He hummed and looked Cook up and down. "The shoddy look works for our friend the cook, but you are an alchemist. They require a bit more direction in their appearance to make any other unusual choices stand out less." He very pointedly did not look toward Mel, who stuck their tongue out at him.

"Be nice," Cook warned. "The captain likes this one."

"Her lovely braids and dashing collection of coats will not persuade me to spare the boy."

"Then at least wait to bother him until he's not a paying customer," Mel snapped. They turned to me, an unholy glint in their eye as they sipped from their canister. "Now, drink your coffee so we can get down to business. Or do you prefer tea?"

My mouth worked open and closed several times before I could answer. "Coffee's fine." I preferred tea for relaxing, but this was a work event, and that meant coffee. Also, Cook had warned me about their tea. I grabbed one of the three mugs left behind—a chipped blue one with ornate Celtic creatures painted in and around it—and filled it with my preferred blend of coffee, milk, and sugar.

Mel grumbled about blasphemous beverages under their breath as we drank. I very nearly agreed with them. Whoever was in charge of the coffee evidently preferred it strong enough to blind a mule. The only thing the sugar did was hide the bitterness behind a thin curtain, and the milk lightened the color but not the grinds.

Still, I choked it down and refused a refill as politely as I could.

Once Cook and Elle set down their mugs, Mel leaped to their feet and clapped, nearly knocking the table over. "Excellent, with those annoying social niceties done, let's get to work. Cook, the list?" He passed it over, and Mel cackled like a banshee at his resigned expression. "Pishposh, you're acting like I'll turn this one into a newt."

"Can you do that?" I asked, getting to my feet. Transformation potions were notoriously difficult, and that was when using standard alchemical processes and reagents. They were, presumably, using anything they could stuff into a teapot. Either tea was an unappreciated vessel for potionwork, or Mel hadn't always been in that field.

"Not anymore." They examined the list and nodded slowly. "The master took away my essence of moonlight and my cat's-cradle." Looking up again, they tossed the list at me and then crossed to the garden half of the room. "Come along, we'll need to work fast to get all this done before closing. Mind the jasmine!"

Cook shoved me after them. "Go along, lad, I've got business to discuss with Konstantyn. We'll be along shortly."

Mel tossed me a set of shears. "You can take the plant life. I'll handle the chemicals."

Nodding, I glanced down at the list for the first time to see what plants I actually needed.

Hakim's lists were always efficient and orderly. This one was no different. Ten different common herbs to restock our stores and a handful of chemical and magical reagents, only half of which I recognized. Furrowing my brow, I frowned.

"Moonsbane?"

"A stone used to predict the arrival of winter and storms," Mel called. The only part of their body still visible was their legs, which were hanging over the edge of a large wooden bin. "Ancient Gothic mages used them in tracking spells. They went out of fashion—" They cut themselves off with a gleeful shout. "I knew I still had some."

They pulled themselves out and frowned to see me still standing where they'd left me. "Well, hurry up. We'll be waiting all day if that's your trimming technique."

Galvanized—and perhaps a little shamed—into action, I leaped to gather the ingredients I recognized. As I worked, I had to admire the efficiency of Mel's garden. Countless plants were crammed in alongside one another. Some bloomed out of season, some right alongside plants they'd wipe out in the wild, and some I knew I'd never find anywhere but here. The sheer variety combined with the relatively little sunlight they must get in a greenhouse in the middle of the city must mean Mel spent a decent portion of their profits on maintaining the spellwork to keep all this running.

Periodically, my musings and gathering were interrupted by shouts and groans from the sitting area.

Glancing over revealed that Konstantyn was pulling items from Elle's sack one at a time and appraising them. From the few items I saw, there wasn't a rhyme or reason to his choices. A golden necklace with a glimmering emerald hanging from it was tossed over his shoulder, but a rusted and stained knife was set on the table with all the respect of a clergyman holding high mass.

He finished with Elle's bag at roughly the same time Mel and I finished gathering the items on Hakim's list. Mel gently wrapped a glass jar of powdered lemon's wort in wax paper and unceremoniously shoved it into my now-bulging satchel alongside the dried wormstongue and the fresh-cut plants I'd gathered.

"That should be everything," Mel said, buckling the straps. "And I believe your cook has one more item he wants us to see."

"Two," Konstantyn called. "He's been fiddling with them for the past half hour."

"And here I thought I was being subtle." Cook passed the bracelets over to Konstantyn, who examined them closely. "I need to know how much power these can hold before they shatter."

Mel snorted, then plopped onto the couch beside Cook. "I suppose you'll be wanting me to cast that enchantment when he's done, then?" They pulled their canteen out and took a long drink. "That'll be extra, you know."

I gently set the satchel on the ground and slid into the armchair by Konstantyn, who didn't even look up from the bracelets. "You're a mage too?"

"A hedge witch really." Multicolored lights danced along their fingers, and they smiled softly. "I never held with the royal academies. Besides, I can research teas this way."

Ah, research. That explained it. Mages weren't allowed to experiment with magic outside their bodies. My mother came to St. Bernard for a similar reason. It was perhaps for the best that my youngest sister, Sophia, had no interest in theoretical magic; otherwise she'd never be able to train her innate magic the way she wanted to.

Most folks with enough innate magical ability to become mages worked as them in one field or another. Alchemy was all well and good, but the right spell could do the work of a dozen potions, assuming the caster had the strength to sustain them, or a person willing to lend them their magic by acting as a conduit. Potionwork was the basis of magic, but there was only so much magic in the reagents, heat, and water that a talented alchemist could manipulate before they were drained entirely. The fields were split for a reason and could only go so far by design. The last time anyone was allowed to freely experiment with the great sources of magic in the world, the Flying Isles were created. Power such as that was best limited to safe and acceptable pathways.

Konstantyn sighed. "These are good items. Egyptian, no?"

Cook nodded. "From the stall by the bakery in the market."

"Good craftsmanship there," he muttered. "These will hold enough magic to do what you wish, but only just and because they are a match." He handed the bracelets to Mel, whose pleasant smile dropped as they held them at arm's length. "If one breaks, the spell will shatter, and the conduit—you—will face the consequences."

Cook smiled grimly. "And I will, gladly." He turned to me and nodded. "Why don't you take that to the front? Mel and I will meet you up there in a few minutes."

As much as part of me wanted to stay, I knew better

than that. Magic could be a private thing, and I could see his purse on the table. Whatever this was, it wasn't the business of the ship *Vulturnus*, and there were only a few spells I knew that bore consequences to the one offering up their magic to power them. Whoever was destined for those bracelets was fortunate indeed.

Chapter 3

Cook didn't speak on the walk back to the ship except to direct me one way or the other. Exhaustion lined his frame, from the stoop of his shoulders to the way each step dragged and the heavy catch of his breath. There was no sign of the bracelets, and I wondered if he'd already passed them on. Spells like that weren't meant to be held by the conduit for long, or both would burn out from the strain.

Still, it wasn't my place to ask, so I didn't. If Cook wanted me to know, he'd tell me.

The streets were darkening by the time we reached the docks. The sun had fallen below the waterline, lighting up the clouds and the waves like a fire that consumed the world. Whales swam in and out of a distant thunderhead, dancers of the sky singing their songs to the gulls and the stars. If we'd had time, I would've paused to take it in, but Cook barely broke stride.

The ship waited at the end of the pier, jutting into the evening fog above the smaller fishing boats and interisland ferries around it like a spear. If I squinted, I could just make out someone scrambling through the rigging.

"Hurry up," Cook muttered, his accent thicker than I'd ever heard it. "I'll not be keeping Hakim any longer than necessary, and I've still got a stove waiting for me."

While part of me wanted to snap that I was the one carrying all our purchases, I held my tongue. It was the weight of the spell, I told myself. He'd probably apologize come morning.

But if he kept grumbling like that, I might let loose my tongue.

Fortunately for both Cook and myself, we reached the ship before I lost my temper. There weren't any streetwalkers on board tonight, likely driven off by the weather and the lackluster charms of the crew that hadn't drawn leave tonight, and thus there was no music. The deck itself was empty apart from the watchman currently huddled around a brazier, and a vaguely familiar figure in a rich green cloak.

"You're late." Alice's voice rang out over the ship like an abbey bell over its domain. Sharp, clean, and annoyed that others would dare argue against it.

Cook shrugged. "Konstantyn had another client."

She huffed and then—to my great surprise and embarrassment—removed her cloak and threw it over his shoulders. His surprise matched mine, but likely less because we had never seen her so considerate of others and more because her dark green dress was styled such that even a walker might be embarrassed to be seen in it. Her blond hair was pinned up like a noble woman, and she'd spread some manner of red paint over her lips.

"Oh, be quiet. I'm headed to the Dutch quarter tonight, and dressed like this, no one will notice me slipping in among all the other streetwalkers."

Alice handled the less savory contacts and information gathering for Captain Proulx. She knew every back alley bar and drunken scoundrel in Fortitude like the back of her hand if even half the rumors were true. Our latest commission must involve the Dutch in some way or other.

But then Cook did something that shocked me even more than Alice's outfit had. He *growled*. "Give me ten minutes. I'll come with you."

Snorting, Alice slapped him upside the head. "No, I'm

supposed to be working. Can't do that if you're scowling at all my contacts." She paused and looked me up and down. "He's in one piece and the same color as when he left. Mel must've liked him."

"He did all right," Cook allowed, a scowl still darkening his face.

I coughed. "Um, not to interrupt, but where's the quartermaster?" The pressure of the satchels cutting into my shoulders had been steadily growing since we left the Swoop, but it was intolerable now that we were on board and relief waited moments away. Besides, they could continue their lovers' quarrel once I was out of the way.

Alice let out a low laugh. "He's in with the captain. Head on down to your storeroom, I'll let him know you're back." Scowling at Cook, she made as to take her cloak back, but he stepped back and waggled his eyebrows at her. "As for you, if you're going to keep that, you should head down to the kitchen. The others want their dinner."

With little recourse—and no desire to get in between them more than necessary—I followed behind them. They continued their rapid-fire bickering all the way through the hold and only separated at the galley door. Cook returned her cloak with a vulgar gesture, took the satchels with his purchases, and entered the galley to a roar of cheers.

Alice slipped away, racing above deck and wrapping her cloak around her bare shoulders as she went, and I was left alone.

What did Kit do when they were like this? If I had to put up with that, I'd move out. Say what you will for Alderman's snoring, at least it didn't make me feel like the odd wheel on a wonky wagon.

The storeroom was hidden behind a stack of crates. Any good privateer had someplace for their alchemist to hide away, lined with metal and far from the powder room lest an errant blaze or spark of magic found its way into the wrong barrel.

The *Vulturnus*'s storeroom was well equipped, even for a privateer. The space wasn't large enough for the tools I'd had when I lived with my mother, but it had enough to do my job and dozens of drawers to hold my reagents. Hakim had even graciously given me leave to use the journals and textbooks left behind by the previous alchemist—God rest her soul and may the Spanish bastards that killed her fall to a pox—until I was able to assemble my own collection.

Hakim entered as I sorted through the last of our purchases. I hadn't put anything away yet, since Hakim preferred to account for what entered the ship himself, but they were orderly. And plentiful. Once emptied, the contents of my satchel covered the whole of my worktable.

"Edward." Hakim moved as silent as a baby's breath, and it was only because I'd been facing the door that I knew he had entered at all. "Were you able to get everything?"

Nodding, I gestured to our haul. "I needed to gather some of them myself, but the Swoop's proprietor had the entire list."

He hummed and ran his fingers over the jars and packages. "So I see." He lingered over the barley seeds, his eyes hollow, before he looked back to me. "What did you think of Mel? They're an odd duck, that's for certain."

I shrugged. "I've met stranger." Mother's old school friends came to mind. One had spent his entire trip huddled over our latest clutch of chicks, explaining in detail the various characteristics of their droppings and feathers to Sophia. Another took our best teapot and brewed a liquor strong enough to knock even my drunkard of a father on his back. They'd then used that concoction to water the roses, which have bloomed purple ever since.

"Good. Most who meet them either come back with new appendages or scared out of their wits by their curse checker." He chortled and clapped me on the shoulder. "Alice says Cook was impressed with you. The next time we're in port, I'll send you directly to the Swoop and have another hand help with the shopping. It would do you good to visit with an alchemist like Mel more often."

I opened my mouth to protest, but he spoke again before I could.

"Right, get all this put away and then you're done for the night. You're welcome to go ashore if you want. It'll be a while before we make port again."

He was gone before I finished nodding, leaving me with the reagents and the rocking of the waves.

The faint smell of stew reached my nose as I put the last of the purchases away, and my stomach rumbled. The pie from this afternoon felt as far away as St. Bernard, and my purse was much lighter than it had been this morning.

I slammed the last drawer shut and rushed to the door, the empty satchel thrown over my shoulder to return to Cook. I cast one last look back to confirm everything was locked and neatly stored, and paused on the threshold.

The drawer I stored the barley seeds in was open . . . and the seeds were gone.

***

The morning came quickly and with it, news of our latest commission.

Kit gathered the crew, a bedraggled group that was hungover and still drunk in turns, on deck under the light of the rising sun and what little fog hadn't been burned off yet for an address from Captain Proulx.

She and Hakim huddled together on the upper deck,

fervently arguing about something I had no chance of understanding down here. The rising noises of the dock blocked out any sound that might have made the distance. Finally, the captain pushed Hakim back and strode to the railing.

She stared at us from under the brim of her hat, a rather fetching red tricorne with a griffin feather stuck through the brim, and frowned. "Gentlefolk," she began, hooking her thumbs through her belt. "As you've no doubt heard, I've accepted a commission."

Normally, such a pronouncement was followed by an explanation, but none seemed to be forthcoming. And also normally, she'd have asked for the crew's opinion on the commission before she accepted it.

"Due to the nature of the commission and the one offering it, I can't risk giving details about it until we're out of port, but I will say that this may very well be one of our more dangerous and profitable adventures." Her eyes lingered on some of the newer crewmembers, myself among them. "If you feel you cannot accept the risks without more knowledge, you're free to stay in Fortitude, and we'll pick you up on the return journey, but doing so will forfeit any percentage of the prize money."

That drew a thunder of grumbles from even the drunker of the crew, and I found myself thrumming with excitement. I labored under no delusion that I'd be one of those who stayed behind. I was here to earn money, and I trusted the captain to not lead me into a situation where I had no chance of escaping.

And if, by chance, she did, I knew she was the sort of person to make sure my portion of the prize money made it back home.

Hakim strode up to Captain Proulx's side, his eyes shrouded in darkness. "Anyone who wishes to leave will need to speak with me. We're shoving off within the hour."

Thus dismissed, the crew mostly split into small groups, and two hands went directly to Hakim. For my part, I went downstairs to double-check my herb supply. We restocked yesterday, but it didn't hurt to make sure we didn't need anything more.

Gossip filtered into the storeroom on each draft of air. Some of the other crewmembers wondered out loud what kind of commission the captain had accepted. Secrets, as many pointed out, were beyond our pay grade. None doubted we were capable of rising to the challenge, but the more cautious ones reminded the rest that we were used to calmer work.

Most of the crew was content to trust the captain and Hakim to see us through, and as I counted myself among their number, I didn't pay much attention to those that didn't.

Beyond the barley seeds, which were easily replaceable, I was set for a long voyage. Mentally, I went over the sky charts and plotted out which islands we might be passing by and what plant life they were known to contain in the event I'd need more reagents.

The door creaked shut, and I caught a flash of red in the corner of my eye. I looked up to greet my visitor and tripped over my tongue. "I'm not—" My words fled for a half a heartbeat before I remembered myself. "Ah, hello, Fan Ju. Did you need something?"

She smiled pleasantly and nodded. She wore plain linen trousers, like those I'd seen on other Liúwáng folk, over a red linen shirt, and a heavy leather apron on top of that. A pair of ivory pins stuck out of a loose bun that sent cascades of dark brown hair down to frame her long—and slightly gray—face. "Yes, hello."

I could count on one hand the number of times I'd spoken with Fan Ju since I came on board, and I'd spoken with her husband, Yunru, even less. They rarely needed my assistance, preferring their own alchemy when necessary. I will admit, I'd been quite pleased with this arrangement, so seeing her in my storeroom was both unexpected and unusual.

"I need something for nausea. My husband is restocking our supplies, but we are out of ginger tea."

Nausea, right, that was easy. "Sure, I've got something for that hanging around." Ginger was easy enough and we had plenty of it. Hakim had ordered a triple supply for some reason, and it had barely fit into its cabinet. If I mixed in some dried chamomile, it would help it go down easier. "Just nausea?"

Best to ask, as my mother had always drilled into me. There might've been something that patients were holding back either out of embarrassment or forgetfulness.

"Nothing that ginger couldn't cure," she said in a soft voice. "You are good to ask. Too many of your tradesfolk assume they know better."

I let out a nervous laugh as I started chopping the ginger. "That's what my mother always says. She taught me well."

Fan Ju walked to the edge of my table and sank into my chair. "Your mother? You learned at her knee? Our last alchemist was self-taught."

But well-informed, or so the books she left behind suggested. "Aye. She provides potionwork and healing for most of the smaller islands around our home."

"And you went to fly instead of helping her?"

I nodded. The ginger was almost done, and I grabbed a jar of chamomile. I offered it to Fan Ju for inspection, and she smiled.

"Yes. Someone had to. We needed the money." My father couldn't, and Oliver was content enough in his apprenticeship with the baker even if he had any inclination toward the mortar and pestle.

"Who helps her now?" Fan Ju turned a little green, and I rushed through the final stages. Polite conversation was good and all, but it shouldn't be dawdled over if the patient looked ill.

"My younger sister, Felicity, took over the apprenticeship when I became a journeyman." And fancied herself better at it than me within a few months, since she could pull more power from her reagents than I could. Mother was quick to remind her that innate magical ability wasn't worth squat if you couldn't name most herbs and struggled to remember to turn the burner off. I poured my mixture into a pouch made of wax paper and smiled cheerfully. "Here you go, this is enough for a few pots at least."

Fan Ju took it and pushed herself up. Her smile was noticeably smaller. "Will you go back when your sister's apprenticeship is done?"

My eyebrows jumped up. "Are you that eager to get rid of me?" The tone was joking, but a sharp stab of fear tied my stomach in knots. No captain worth their salt would unnecessarily anger their Liúwáng engineers. If Fan Ju or Yunru wanted me gone, Captain Proulx would see it done, hang whatever agreement she'd made with my mother.

My father had learned that the hard way, and he'd drilled that into my head from the day the merchant ships started resupplying in St. Bernard. You did not upset the Liúwáng if you wanted to sail in the sky. Everyone knew it and everyone lived by that law. Doing so was the end of the matter as far as the world was concerned. The one who caused offense would be exiled and the ones who dared love them would be forced to bear the weight of that punishment until their dying day. There was a reason I didn't use my father's name.

She let out a bark of laughter that did absolutely nothing to soothe my nerves. "No, but you seem like a dutiful son. I've seen how you attend to lessons from Mr. Kit and Mr. Hakim. Your parents must miss you."

"Parent," I said before I could stop myself. To cover it, I sped onward. "It's just my mother and my siblings back home. My father isn't—"

She cut me off before I could dig myself even deeper into this hole. "Ah, my apologies. You left to support them, then? I cannot imagine that there's enough work for one skilled alchemist on most islands in the southern sky, let alone two."

The words were accurate enough, if not quite the entire truth. Nonetheless, I was happy to take the escape route they offered. "Yes. My siblings help with the farm, but when my youngest sister, Sophia, said she wanted to go to a mainland academy, I knew I'd have to find work elsewhere to help her get there."

The farm could support a family of six easily enough, and even comfortably when my mother and I had plentiful work, but the academy strained merchants pockets. Even with my contributions, Sophia would still need a sponsor. I just hoped my wages would give her more choice in the matter of whose offer she accepted.

Fan Ju patted my hand once more and took the tea. "You are a dutiful son," she repeated. Her eyes grew damp and she sniffled. "I'm certain you make your mother proud, and I know we are fortunate to have you with us."

She darted out before I could stop her, tearing around sailors and supplies with the ease of one raised on these ships. The door to her quarters slammed shut just as I reached the hold. One of the sailors glanced at me from the corner of their eye and made a sign to ward off evil.

I could have defended myself, but I knew better than to try. There were few things that looked worse than one of the engineers fleeing from you. I uttered several words I wouldn't admit to knowing if my mother had been here, and gingerly closed the storeroom door behind me. I could apologize later, I told myself as queasiness tied my stomach in knots. I would make amends without question once I figured out what I'd done to cause such a reaction in the first place.

***

True to Captain Proulx's wishes and Hakim's words, we shoved off at the hour. A handful of the crew had stayed behind, but there were plenty of us left to fill the shifts.

Fortitude faded into the distance behind us and then disappeared entirely when we passed through a bank of clouds. Fan Ju never emerged from her quarters, although Yunru stomped above deck not long after we'd left. Enerick, the crewmember who was helping me with my chores in the rigging today, pointed him out to me from our position in the rigging. She was a short and muscular fae woman with long pointed ears, a thick beard, and skin that vaguely resembled elmwood. She'd been wandering the skies since before I was born, and allegedly held a dubious reputation among her kin for her willingness to associate and work with humans, which was rare for any of fae blood. Overhead, the griffins squabbled over portions of meat, and the sounds produced by them eating their breakfast did nothing for my stomach.

"Wonder what's got him out and about," Enerick muttered under her breath, stroking her beard. "He normally can't be pulled from below deck unless we've laid anchor somewhere."

I shrugged in lieu of answering, my odd conversation with Fan Ju running through my mind. Whatever magic kept the ship up and thrummed through each board, rope, and nail was also temperamental. There was a reason engineers traveled in groups of two or three. For Yunru to leave his quarters now meant he feared something worse than the ship potentially falling from the sky.

Heavy tools weighed down Yunru's belt, holding the sturdy leather in place even as the wind whipped the loose ends of his shirt and trousers around like kites. His gaze wandered the deck and the sails, lingering on Enerick and me before he darted to Hakim.

My stomach sunk lower still, and bile rose in the back of my throat.

Surely Yunru wouldn't demand my removal over an offense unknowingly given. The others always said he was a fair man and surprisingly open for an engineer newly exiled from China. According to rumor, most new Liúwáng saw offense around every corner. Sailors and alchemists alike saw their livelihoods ruined by a single wrong word or the tiniest offense given to a wrong person. I resolved to beg for his forgiveness as soon as my feet hit the deck.

I hurried through my chores in the riggings as fast as I dared and Enerick would let me. Several times, she forced me to redo my knots or adjust my position until she was satisfied. As she put it, the engineers may have made the ship fly, but they still needed the ship in good repair to keep it up.

My eyes wandered to Hakim and Yunru often as I worked, and I paid for inattention with bruised knuckles and ears ringing with Enerick's cursing, but I couldn't help it. We were much too far to hear a word they said or make out their expressions, but their bodies spoke loudly for all to see. Hakim's shoulders tensed, energy with no outlet coiling in each limb, and while Yunru rarely moved more than necessary, it was echoed in the frantic twitching of his hands while they spoke.

As if they sensed my eyes upon them, they looked up at me, and I nearly fell from the rigging. Only Enerick's quick hands saved me.

"Did you leave your head in Fortitude?" she snapped. She ran a hand through her braided hair and sighed. "By the isles, you're jumpier than a pig at the butcher's today."

"Sorry," I said faintly, clinging tightly to the rigging. "Must've been something I ate."

Enerick shook her head. "Queasy stomach or no, you won't make it in the skies if you can't stay in the riggings." She followed my gaze, once more locked on Hakim and Yunru, and sighed. "Whatever you're worried about, it can wait until we're out of the rigging. Pay attention now, we're almost done."

Despite the harshness of her words, she didn't lecture me or make me redo any more knots to meet her standard of perfection. We scrambled down from the riggings a few minutes later, and Hakim called my name at nearly the same moment my feet touched the deck.

Enerick gave me a pitying look and pat my hip. "It'll be fine, Edward," she said, her smile too forced to be comforting. "Go speak with him, it cannot be as bad as you fear."

Swallowing, I tried to take her words to heart even if it was clear she didn't believe them herself.

Hakim waited for me by the stairs to the lower decks. There was no sign of Yunru. Hakim jerked his head back as soon as I drew close enough to hear him. "Follow me, this is a conversation better suited for the stateroom than the open deck."

My heart plummeted from my chest and continued through the deck toward the water far below. "Sir?"

He didn't answer me. My feet clung to the deck like iron clung to a magnet, but I followed him nonetheless. I didn't try to ask him questions, for fear of worsening whatever awaited me there. I didn't dare dawdle for the same reason.

The hold was empty apart from us. The others either slept in the crew's quarters or were hard at work above us. A part of me felt grateful beyond reckoning that there was no one else to lay witness to what surely must be Hakim and Captain Proulx's punishment for whatever I'd done to offend Fan Ju. I just hoped I'd still be able to work once all was said and done. The consequences of offending the Liúwáng were the subject of many a late-night tale in the taverns and below deck, not to mention my family's experiences with their wrath.

By the isles, I knew more stories about people who'd had their entire lives destroyed by merely being related to one who'd angered the Liúwáng than I had hairs on my head. My own name could very well end up among their number if I couldn't figure out how to apologize to Fan Ju before I was kicked off the ship.

Seemingly unaware of my inner turmoil, Hakim led me through the hold and into Captain Proulx's stateroom. The captain herself was nowhere to be seen, and my anxiety cooled into a solid lump in my stomach. I didn't know if that was a good or bad sign, but it meant something.

Hakim finally turned, and his face was grayer than usual. After shutting the door behind him and locking it, he gingerly sat in one of the tall chairs and indicated I take the one across from him. My legs trembled beneath me like hot wax in a strong breeze. The short trip to the other side of the table might as well have been a marathon from one side of the Atlantic Sky to the other, but one sharp look from Hakim sent me scurrying there.

He sighed and rubbed his face. His beard had lost its characteristic shine, and many of its loose braids disappeared in the frazzled whole, I noted as I hid my shaking hands beneath the table.

Tension tightened his shoulders, and he rubbed his eyes. "This doesn't leave these walls until I say so, understand?" he said with a growl. "Yunru didn't want to tell anyone yet, but Fan Ju insisted you know."

"I didn't mean to offend her." The words spilled out of me like wine spilled from an overturned glass. "I don't know what I did, but I promise I'll make it up to her."

Hakim's eyebrows shot up to his hairline. "Offend her? What're you talking about?"

My tongue caught in my throat. "I . . . I . . . Isn't this about Fan Ju running from the storeroom this morning? She came to me for tea, and we were talking, but she started crying and"—now that the plug was pulled, the words couldn't be stopped, an endless torrent as certain as the wind that blew us across the sky—"I tried to catch her but I couldn't and I'm not sure what happened but please don't exile me, I need this job and—"

"Edward," Hakim snapped, "calm down, you're not in trouble."

My jaw slammed shut so hard, the clack must've been audible from across the room. If I hadn't been sitting already, I may have keeled over. As it was, it took a not-unnoticeable period of time for me to find my tongue again. "I'm not?"

Hakim shook his head. "No. The opposite, in fact. Fan Ju has requested your help with an ongoing delicate matter."

"She has?" I sat up straight, adrenaline flooding through my limbs. When it combined with my lingering anxiety, I wanted to throw up. "But why? She knows as much herblore as I do."

Chinese alchemy had different focuses than European alchemy, but the one thing we agreed on was the importance of herblore and chemistry. Fan Ju was more than capable of supplying the ship with all the potions and remedies its crew needed if she hadn't needed those same skills to keep the ship and her husband running.

Bloody hell, the only way I was more skilled than her was as a surgeon, and she had practically glowed with health when I saw her this morning. Whatever she needed must be—

"She's pregnant."

I looked at Hakim and he looked at me. My mouth moved soundlessly, shaping words I couldn't find the air to speak.

"Pregnant?" I finally managed, my head drifting with the shifting of the ship. God, at least that explained the missing barley seeds. Fan Ju must've wanted to make sure she was pregnant before she told the captain. "How?"

He snorted. "You're a grown man, surely I don't need to explain how children are made."

"But . . ." Everyone knew that the Liúwáng took care of their own. We were close enough to Fortitude for Captain Proulx to turn this ship around and return Fan Ju to her own people until she gave birth. "You know what'll happen to us, to *me*, if she miscarries."

I'd never work on a ship again. The Liúwáng would make sure of it. If something happened to her, I'd be lucky if the Liúwáng just exiled me. With the merchant's brand on my forehead, I'd probably be kicked out of the alchemists guild, and no reputable village would want me within a dozen miles of their weak and sickly. By the isles, it might stroke my ego to know that she trusted me enough to want my help with a delicate matter like this, but I'd rather be less self-confident and still have my job.

Hakim set a heavy hand on my shoulder, and it did little to stop my heavy panting.

"It'll be fine. She said she trusts you."

"But can't we go back to Fortitude?" I managed. My voice squeaked like a teenager, and I wasn't ashamed. "There's still time. She not nearly far enough along—"

"She asked for you specifically," Hakim said, his deep voice cutting through my suddenly boyish one like the ship cut through the clouds. "I didn't ask why, but she and Yunru want you to do this and not whoever's waiting for them back in Fortitude. Whatever happens, they'll be on your side before the tribunal."

My side. Yeah right. All that meant was they might let me ride back to Fortitude before exiling me from their ship.

"But . . ." All my words had fled out the stateroom window and refused to return.

Hakim's eyes softened. "It'll be all right. If the winds are with us, we'll be back long before you need to do more than make her the occasional anti-nausea potion."

God, I hoped so. I hadn't assisted with a birth in nearly a year.

"She'll be coming to you in a few days. In the meantime, read up on your midwifery."

***

My nerves hadn't settled by the time Captain Proulx and Hakim called the crew to the galley to discuss the nature of our commission after dinner.

I was fortunate enough to find a space on a bench to

squeeze onto. The galley wasn't meant to hold the whole crew at once, and it was tight. Every flat surface had a butt on it, and the tables had four or five, including Enerick, who flashed me a smile as I sat down.

Captain Proulx stood at the front of the galley, her braids done up in an elaborate bun on top of her head and her coat pulled snugly across her body. Her frown got deeper still as she observed us. Hakim set a supportive hand on her shoulder, and she covered it with hers. The crew's chatter died down to an expectant silence. She did not disappoint nor did she mince words.

"The master of Fortitude has hired us to rob a Dutch merchant." She paused and took a deep breath, looking unsure for the first time I'd ever seen. "Specifically, the Van der Berg trading company."

The outcry was immediate and deafening. Half the seated crew took to their feet, and the ones already standing raised their voices to be heard. My heart dropped to my stomach, and I took in a ragged gasp. Bad enough that Fan Ju wanted me to help with her pregnancy, but to do it on a job like this? I was practically signing my death warrant.

The Van der Bergs were one of the wealthiest merchants in this hemisphere and were based out of an island chain called the Seven Brothers that floated over the Netherlands. There were mainland kings that had less influence than them. More coin passed through their hands than most countries collected in annual taxes. They had hundreds of ships under their control, thousands of sailors in their employ, and regularly sponsored mages at the Dutch academy. To rob them was to gain the enmity of the most powerful organization outside of Fortitude itself.

"Quiet," Hakim yelled, banging his fist against the

galley door. "Let the captain speak."

The shouting died down, but the simmering anxiety beneath it did not. I wasn't the only one panicking about what this would mean, and Hakim couldn't stem those whispers.

Captain Proulx waited for everyone to take their seats again before she continued, "I know how it sounds, but there is a silver lining." Her voice was steady and firm, the soothing nature of her words belied by the monotone of the tongue delivering them. "The master swore that the Van der Bergs robbed him recently, and he wants us to recover his property for him."

The explanation continued, and by turns my stomach rose and fell.

The master had reached out to Alice not long after we docked, and from there arranged a meeting with Captain Proulx and Hakim. During that meeting, he'd hinted at the time-sensitive nature of this mission and ended it by producing a blood-bound contract and promising a high enough sum to buy three ships twice the size of the *Vulturnus* if Captain Proulx returned with his property by the agreed upon date and half that if we returned afterward. She paused then, words caught on her tongue and a strange look on her face.

Hakim took the opportunity to assure the crew that they would receive their contracted parts of the prize in full and bonuses for extraordinary work, and my jaw dropped.

A single portion of that reward was more than my mother would earn in three months. The thoughts of the other crewmembers followed that bend, and the whispers that had bordered on mutinous a few minutes ago turned welcoming. All that and a promise we'd be safe from any retribution when we returned? That was a hard bargain to turn down.

"We understand that this is a lot to ask you, but we can't risk the Van der Bergs finding out. If any of you have reconsidered, we'll drop you off at a nearby island and pick you up after the job's done. If we don't return in two months, the master will send someone to retrieve you."

No one took the offer, the tantalizing thought of the coin that awaited success more appealing than waiting on an island, unable to find any sort of work in the meantime. Whispers and quiet conversation filled the air as the crew filed out, and I followed, deep in thought.

One of these events was hard enough. But both? Whatever happened on this journey might very well ruin me.

Chapter 4

Once a week or so, I drew the night watch. Normally, I didn't mind. Sure, I'd be tired the next day, and I'd miss whatever entertainment Cook dreamed up in the galley, but it was peaceful, and the view of the stars was second to none. Once the sun set and the only light came from cracks in the deck, it honestly felt like I could fall off the horizon and escape into the heavens. Some days, that was more appealing than others.

But right now it was cold and miserable. We'd been bouncing above and below the cloudline, running from a storm while trying to make best use of the winds. Right now, a dark thunderhead that hadn't quite broken yet lumbered above us, blocking all those lovely stars from view, and the lingering thrum of lightning within them made the air feel greasy and thick. The wind picked up not long after sunset, and the creaking of the sails was my only company in this darkness.

At least I had the lamps to tend on a night like tonight. There wasn't much to do beside keep them lit and squint into the darkness for ships like ours and approaching sky life. Without the stars, one of those was a much greater danger than others, and the wind ripped any whale song away before we had a chance to hear it. At least ships would have lights if their sailors had any sense in their heads. A whale would ruin the ship and barely notice.

The door to the lower decks creaked open as I was squinting into a nearby cloud, trying to decide if the shadow I saw was just that or a dolphin pod. Likely just a shadow, I finally decided as it danced across the clouds. Dolphins normally held their place better than that.

"Is all well?" Hakim's voice erupted from the shadows, and I nearly leaped out of my skin.

"Ah, yes sir," I managed to say, shoving my hands into my pockets to hide their shaking. By the isles, I hadn't been expecting that. "All's quiet above and below."

He stepped out of the shadow and into the light of the lookout lamp. "Good to hear. The sky life is more active in weather like this."

I made an agreeing noise and glanced back to the sky. "Did you need something, sir?" My mind whirled. Normally when someone came out when I was on shift, something had gone horribly wrong. Once, someone had gotten stabbed at a card game gone wrong. Another time, half the crew came down with food poisoning a day out of port. We'd gone through my entire stock of blackberry leaves, stems, and roots during that episode, and I hadn't been able to eat porridge for weeks afterward. No one ever just came to chat with me while I was on watch.

He shrugged and warmed his hands on the lamp. "No reason. I gave second shift the night off and thought I'd come out to keep you company."

Ah, marital problems. As quartermaster, Hakim was exempt from watch duty unless he didn't want to be. He and Captain Proulx must've had an argument because no one in their right mind would want to stand watch when they had a warm bed and a friendly ear waiting for them.

"Problems in your cabin, sir?" Buoyed by the indifference and poor thinking of youth, the words fled my mouth before my common sense could pull them back.

Hakim let out a sharp laugh. "Let's just say it's warmer out here right now."

Thanking God that he'd found my poor attempt at humor amusing, I forced out a chuckle. "Bad luck there, sir. Dare I ask why?"

Why wasn't I stopping? We'd had a small joke, and now we could keep staring into the distance. This close, I could smell the lingering remnants of the incense we had burned when Hakim and I prepared this afternoon's tracking spells.

"Oh, you know, standard things for a captain and first mate to argue about. The ship, the crew, the engineers, *you*—"

"Me?" My eyebrows shot up, and I spared a thought to be glad of my hat for hiding it. "Why me?"

He shrugged and then pulled his jacket tighter around himself when the wind sharply increased. "You don't like being alone with the engineers."

Well, Hakim was never one to pull punches.

"That's not true." I actually liked them the few times we'd interacted. Yunru had an incredibly dry sense of humor when faced with something foolish, and Fan Ju was an incredible alchemist. If they hadn't been Liúwáng or I hadn't been the son of an exile, we probably could've been friends. It was just . . . Well, considering who my father was and the brand he bore, I couldn't afford to get too close to them without putting my career at risk. I'd gone too far as it was, but I couldn't make myself stop now without drawing even more attention to my family's history with the Liúwáng. "They're good people."

"And yet, you fought against treating Fan Ju." He didn't look at me, just shifted until his bulky frame no longer blocked the wind.

The wind bit into my exposed skin, and I hunkered down into the scant warmth offered by my scarf. "It's complicated."

Hakim chuckled. "More complicated than helping a young couple with their pregnancy?"

A choked laugh burst from my throat. "You have no idea."

He crouched next to me, his frame blocking out the wind once more. The space between us became an oasis of calm, one perfect for secret conversations. "Then tell me," he said in a low voice. "Make me understand why this is complicated."

My heart leaped into my throat, and the urge to come clean swept through me like a hurricane swept the water below us. I wanted to tell him, to share the secret hanging from my shoulders, but did I dare? If it were just me, if my mother weren't depending on my pay to get Sophia into school, I'd have told him in a heartbeat. Hakim was a good man, for all he was a privateer and occasional marauder—not that I had any room to talk—and more than that, I wanted to trust him.

The weight in my chest made the decision for me. "Please, you can't tell anyone. My family's counting on me. I need this job."

He raised an eyebrow and cast a quick glance around him. The wind and the rain had driven other crew below deck, but still he came closer and lowered his voice. "Edward, what is it? Debtors? Unwanted suitors? The captain and I can help—"

"It's my father," I said all in a rush. The words had left me like a tidal wave, and my limbs shook in their wake. "He's—" But I couldn't say it. My tongue froze and my throat closed.

"Edward?" Hakim whispered. His warm hand settled on my shoulder. The wind carried the lingering smell of smoke and incense from the ritual forward. My mother always smelled like that. It lingered like nothing else. "Are you all right?"

"He was exiled," I whispered, sinking into my scarf. It was done. The news was out, and it was up to Hakim to decide what to do with it. "He got drunk and robbed an engineer, and they branded him—"

Hakim's hand slammed over my mouth. "Enough." His voice shook, and he glanced around furtively, like someone could've approached in the brief time since last he looked. "An exile? You're sure?"

I wanted to give him a withering glare, but my better sense grabbed onto that urge and throttled it. No one with any sense would admit to being related to an exile if they wanted to keep working on Liúwáng ships. Half the sailors in St. Bernard had been too terrified to visit Mother for potions and healing, as if my father's sins would rub off on them and see them exiled too. The only reason my mother had been able to get me this job was that my father passed away last winter and the villagers had begun softening toward us without him there to remind them of his crimes.

Hakim's hand dropped, and he rubbed it over his eyes. "No wonder you didn't want to help," he muttered. "By the isles, that puts you in a tough spot." The wind howled behind him, and he shivered. When his eyes next met mine, his jaw set, and he seemed to make a decision. "You should've told us earlier. The captain doesn't need this stress right now."

If the deck had swallowed me whole at this very moment, I'd have gone gladly. Since it stubbornly refused to oblige, I was forced to face the moment, and my fists shook. This was it. He'd tell the captain, she'd tell Yunru and Fan Ju, and they'd demand I be exiled, too, because the Liúwáng guarded their secrets closer than a queen guarded her jewels and my family was irrevocably tainted.

I'd never be able to work on another ship again. My sister would never attend the academy. I'd failed them, and it was my own fault for not keeping my mouth shut.

Hakim smiled softly and ruffled my hair. If I hadn't been on the verge of a breakdown, it would've felt patronizing. "You're a good lad, and your father's mistakes aren't yours. I trust you not to harbor resentment toward the Liúwáng for someone else's actions."

My heart froze, and my brain refused to comprehend what he was saying. "Sir?"

"You heard me."

I . . . had. He wasn't going to tell Fan Ju or Yunru about my father. My lips spread in a huge smile, and only the vaguest sense of propriety kept me from launching myself at Hakim for a hug.

"Than—thank you, sir," I stuttered. "I won't let you down."

He trusted me. That shouldn't have been as much of a shock as it was. I was the one helping Fan Ju through her pregnancy, and Cook liked me. I had an important job on the crew, and I was willing to work hard to earn my place here.

But it was hard to shake a lifetime of looking over my shoulder for the next person to make a gesture to ward off evil when they looked at my family, and for captains and merchants alike to think twice about working with us. My father had tried to support us before he'd sought salvation in the bottom of the bottle, but most of the villagers refused to buy anything from our farm if they knew he'd touched it. If it hadn't been for my mother's alchemy shop, which was the only one on the island, we'd have starved a dozen times over before I'd begun my apprenticeship.

"You won't, lad." Hakim shook himself and stepped back. "Now, it's nearly the end of your shift, and I'm officially relieving you. Go downstairs and tell Cook to prepare something to warm you up, on my orders."

***

The next few days moved quickly, bolstered by my duties among the crew and my tasks as an alchemist.

First Fan Ju and later Yunru came to speak with me about what Fan Ju would need as her pregnancy progressed.

Fan Ju was more practical about it. She quizzed me about my midwifery experiences, the potions I preferred for nausea and pain, and what I wanted her to do to maintain her health and my sanity the further we got from Fortitude. In turn, once I got over my lingering anxiety to treat the patient in front of me instead of panicking over what it could mean for me, I went over the list of questions for expectant parents my mother had made.

What would make them more comfortable in case the worst happened: a home birth—or in this case, a cabin birth—or a stay in my storeroom to have instant access to my medical supplies? What herbs would she rather I used? How often would she like me to check in?

There was more too. Alchemy might be simple hedge magic, but most alchemists had enough innate magic to cast basic healing spells. I was not so fortunate. Basic diagnostic spells exhausted my abilities most days. Even soothing bruises was beyond me. Was she still comfortable with me as her midwife, knowing we'd need to rely on my stock of potions instead of spells?

She hadn't minded. Oddly, she seemed relieved when she found out I wouldn't be using magic.

Over three hours when I would normally be helping in the rigging, we went over everything I could think of and more that she wanted to know. The only reason we stopped at all was because the noon bell rang, and she'd needed to replace her husband. Just as well. Even if my tired brain had been able to speak more, my hand was so cramped up from note-taking, I wouldn't be able to write.

Yunru came after lunch as I was soaking my hand in a solution to ease the pain from his wife's visit.

To say I hadn't been expecting him would've been an understatement of Herculean proportions. In my few months on the ship, I'd overheard him speak with Captain Proulx, Hakim, and Cook, but I'd never actually spoken to him, let alone been alone with him.

So to see him peek through the door, one hand resting on the frame like he was worried I'd throw him out for daring to enter my domain, sent me leaping to my feet.

"Sir, I—" Unfortunately, in my rush to stand, I knocked over the bowl I'd been using, and the solution spilled onto the floor. I let out a handful of words that would've had my mother washing my mouth out with soap, and grabbed a rag from the table. "Sorry, just—give me a moment."

A pale hand joined me in mopping up the solution, and I blanched.

"You don't have to do that, it's my fault it spilled, I'll be with you in a moment."

Yunru waved my concerns away. "It is . . . all right, yes? That is the word. You were startled." He smiled tentatively when I set the now-empty bowl and soiled rags on the table. "I apologize, I did not mean to be a bother. When my wife—"

"I'll take good care of her, sir," I quickly assured him. My hand twitched toward my notebook and ached for it. "We can go over what she and I spoke about this morning, if you would like."

Some folks were uncomfortable with male midwives, even as alchemists. As my mother liked to say, some folks were incapable of separating the work and general location of labor from the activities that created them. Mainlanders were supposedly even more squeamish, which made me wonder how they accomplished anything at all.

Yunru smiled, and for a moment, he looked less like the intimidating man that I knew kept our ship in the air, and more like a man not much older than me about to have his first child. "That will not be necessary." His voice never got louder than a low whisper. He rose to his feet and folded his hands into his sleeves. "My wife and I have discussed her treatment as much as she desired. I am here for other reasons." He frowned, and his voice took on an edge.

"O-oh?" My voice cracked like a boy a decade younger than myself, and I swallowed before I spoke again. He was here about his wife. The Liúwáng were more egalitarian than even the islanders—or the inhabitants of their ancestral homes in mainland China, if the rumors were to be believed—but only among their own folk. Those not of the Liúwáng would always be under a degree of suspicion. Some of us were under more suspicion than others. "What can I help you with, sir?"

Please don't be here to threaten me, I silently pleaded. I knew better than most the consequences of crossing the Liúwáng and that knowledge weighed me down like an anchor.

His face darkened and my heart stopped. "Allow me to apologize to you," he said, bending his upper body in a gentle bow. "I fear my wife and I have unnerved you with our request. Quartermaster Hakim made us aware of your concerns. I would have approached you sooner had I known."

How many concerns could Hakim have explained to them? He couldn't have actually explained why I was uncomfortable with them, or the depths of the consequences forced upon my father that my whole family still suffered from. One did not cross the Liúwáng and stay in the sky. Only the foolhardy and the skysick stayed in the islands after crossing them.

It was difficult to say which my father had been. He'd never given up hope of sailing again. There didn't exist a word to describe those foolish enough to stay and to raise children under such conditions.

Abruptly, I realized Yunru was still bowing, and my anxiety took on new depths. Everything I'd ever heard about the Liúwáng from Chinese sailors and books said that the clans didn't suffer false pride, and Yunru had bent his neck for long enough. "It's all right," I managed, proud that my voice didn't squeak this time. "Hakim and Fan Ju explained some of your reasons. It just took me off guard, is all."

Yunru raised his head a fraction but didn't stand straight. "She said you spoke of herbs and medicine, not our reasons for putting this weight on your shoulders."

His shoulders slumped, and for a moment, panic seized me when he looked like he intended to bow deeper still. Thankfully, he pulled himself straight. His eyes passed up and down me, wandering around my face and the cabin with an uneasy tilt. "Allow me to rectify that."

"Rectify?" Whatever their reasons for the secrecy around this pregnancy, I wanted no part of it. I would tend to her and that was it. "That's not—"

"It will make things clearer and share the burdens on both your shoulders and ours." His voice shook and he audibly swallowed. He glanced at the chair his wife had formerly occupied. "You are an alchemist. The customs of your guild prevent you from speaking of your client's affairs, correct?"

I bit back a sigh. "Of course, sir," I ground out, politer than I wanted to be. "Within reason, anything said while I am under contract is left between my patient and me."

His shoulders noticeably relaxed and he exhaled. "As we thought. I apologize again, I am not yet familiar with all your customs." His hands shook as he pulled the spare chair over and awkwardly lowered himself into it. "My . . ." He paused, rolling something around in his mouth. "Ah, I forget your word. My wife's mother is important among the Liúwáng. Fan Ju is her only remaining child."

"It's really not—" The less I knew, the better, especially if this was a family concern, but Yunru plowed on as if I hadn't spoken.

"It is," Yunru interrupted. "My wife will not rest easy carrying this on her own, and it is one thing to tell the captain and another to hide it from one such as you."

"So you tell me?" My stomach whirled, and I clenched my pen and notebook tightly to hide the way my hands shook. "You have to know that I can't hide anything from the captain that will endanger the crew."

"It is not—" He breathed deeply and closed his eyes. When he spoke again, his words were weighed down with exhaustion. "The captain knows what I'm about to tell you. The only danger is to Fan Ju and myself, not to the crew, so she allowed this."

"A danger to the engineers is a danger to the crew," I managed to say. Despite my better judgment, my mind swirled with the implications of things that could threaten a pregnant woman and her husband. "And this is a great personal risk to myself as well. It's better for everyone involved that I know only enough to keep Fan Ju healthy and the crew safe."

He let out a huff of laughter. "It is not that kind of danger. Fan Ju is young and healthy, and the crew treats us well. The work you do here will be no different than that of the Liúwáng midwives on Fortitude. No, this is purely an issue with my wife's mother."

I didn't want to know, I didn't want to know, I didn't want to—I shouldn't want to know, but I did.

Sod it, my curiosity had been piqued, and I'd already come this far. I might as well go all in. I deflated and rubbed my forehead. A morose chuckle broke past my lips. What a lovely impression I must be making. My mother would be ashamed. Half of an alchemist's job was to ease anxieties and worries, and even if his face stayed serene, only a fool would deny that Yunru's body thrummed with tension.

"Very well. If there's no real risk to the crew, I'll unburden your shoulders."

He bowed his head. "Thank you."

I waited.

And waited.

Yunru breathed in deeply. Twice, I thought he might start, but the urgency of before seemed to have fled. That, or now that he didn't need to fight with me, he lacked the words.

"My wife had a sister." He didn't look up now that his tongue had been loosed. His eyes stayed focused on the ground, and his hands shifted under his long sleeves. "Had."

Ah.

"My condolences," I said in a low voice.

He shrugged. "You could not have known. It happened a few months after our wedding."

I hesitated. This time my tongue was the one trapped behind my teeth. When I finally freed it, I sighed and lowered my head. "What killed her? A birthing fever? The child?"

69

I hated to ask these questions, but I needed to know, and I doubted Fan Ju would want to speak with me about them. To lose her sister to what she now faced . . .

"Neither."

My head jerked up. "What do you mean?"

His face darkened. "Pirates. I had just completed my apprenticeship, but Min Li's loss shook our clan. She was meant to lead after their mother, you know. The raid was . . . surprising. To lose her to it was even more so."

Even pirates respected the Liúwáng. They needed to. Most relied on the engineers to stay aloft the way the privateers and merchants did, and the few that could afford mages instead wouldn't risk losing access to the Liúwáng for a few pittances of gold.

"What happened?" I asked before I could stop myself. Biting back a curse, I silently berated myself. Their loss was not mine to gossip over. "I mean, after that."

Logically, the rest of the Liúwáng would've pursued the pirates until their heads lined the road to the hall of justice on Fortitude. Any captains in good standing would abandon their respective commissions until vengeance had been dealt and Min Li's body recovered for a proper burial. Their mother—

"Nothing," he whispered, his gaze once more falling to his hands. "It was an accident. The raid happened during a fierce storm, and an explosion killed their griffins. Her partner confirmed that nothing could've been done at the trial. There was no justice to be done after the death price had been paid."

Leaving the Liúwáng without anything to soothe their wounds. Even the most careful crew couldn't avoid accidents.

"And their mother?" I suspected that I knew. A loss like that would make any parent want to keep their remaining children close at hand. Especially when they only had one left.

He raised his head, eyes closed, and took in a deep breath. When he opened his eyes, the softness of a fond memory turned his gaze gentle. "She grieved. She and the clan went through our rituals of loss while I prepared to begin my journeyman travels. When Fan Ju decided she wished to join me, her mother let her go. She just had a few conditions."

That must be the crux of the issue. "Among them she wanted you to return if there were children," I guessed, massaging my temples.

"And I would complete my journeyman and master travels without her." My head shot up and he smiled painfully. "It would not do for the sole heir to be married to a lowly journeyman," he explained. "And, I suspect, her mother does not like me as much as some of the more . . . more established members of the clan. I was only an apprentice when I was exiled, you see. I barely knew enough about the ships to be adopted into the clan, and the only reason we were allowed to wed was that Fan Ju was not the heir."

"Of course." My head throbbed, and I debated the merits of making willow bark tea.

An heiress, a lowly apprentice, and a grieving mother. This had all the makings of a morality play or some poor joke with a crude punch line. Either way, I suspected I'd find myself at the butt of something if things continued along this path.

"How long do you plan to hide it from her?" I asked, shoving down the tight pangs shooting through my chest. "She will notice if Fan Ju returns with a child or if her only child refuses to see her."

Yunru shook his head vehemently. "Of course we plan

71

to tell her," he hissed. "Just not yet. Fan Ju—"

He cut himself off this time. "It is not my story to tell. It is enough to say, we plan on honoring her mother's wishes once this voyage is over. The child should not be here yet."

I raised an eyebrow and crossed my arms. "Do you?"

"Yes, we do." He paused, chewing over his next words. When he spoke again, he looked a little unsure. "I do not know the exact details, but I know we won't be able to hide it for longer than the voyage anyway. Her mother befriended a powerful hedge witch in the city and took that choice from us."

My stomach sank. "What do you mean?"

His eyes cast down, and his hands twitched beneath his sleeves. "If Fan Ju is badly hurt or has cause for a healing spell to be cast upon her, her mother will know the cause and severity of her injury."

And she would send the Liúwáng after us.

Bloody hell.

"That's why she didn't want magic to be used on her." I said slowly, rubbing the bridge of my nose. Something as simple as a diagnostic spell wouldn't trigger spells that complex, but anything greater—even something as simple as healing a scraped knee—would. "She'd be caught right away once the spell detected the magic."

Fan Ju's mother must be tremendously wealthy, even by Liúwáng standards. A skilled hedge witch was a rarity. Most were self-taught and free of the oaths that bound their colleagues in the mainland, which made them capable of producing deadly magics and exceptionally powerful potions. Having access to such power led them down dark paths, and many burned their innate magic out before they could become a large enough threat for the mage academies to go after them.

"But potions won't trigger them," Yunru said urgently. A proud smile spread across his face, and he nodded toward the compartment he shared with Fan Ju. "Even the most complex of magics cannot track something if the conduit conditions aren't met, and the locator spell won't trigger when she drinks something a potion can cure. That is our edge and how we will get through this."

I stared at him for a long while. Slowly, his smile fell away too.

"Are you still confused?" he asked finally. "It is a good plan. Captain Proulx agreed to it, and Quartermaster Hakim agreed that we couldn't afford to turn down this commission."

It rang hollow to me. A sole engineer could fly a ship by themself. It might take longer and would be substantially riskier, but it could be done. Captain Proulx and Hakim both knew the risks of angering the Liúwáng, and Fan Ju's mother was wealthy enough to ensure we would never fly again even if Fan Ju returned in the bloom of health with a bouncing babe in her arms. I wasn't being told everything.

A midwife and alchemist among secrets would end with someone dead.

"No."

"Excellent, I—"

"I don't believe that. There's something else going on here."

Captain Proulx and perhaps Hakim knew the whole truth, but Yunru and Fan Ju were hiding something from me.

Yunru stared at me, his mouth hanging open like a fish. "I don't—I can't—I don't know what you mean," he stammered, shooting to his feet. "We've told you everything and—"

"But you haven't. The captain wouldn't agree to something like this unless there was a bigger reward than you and Fan Ju being together for a bit longer." Calm. Steady. Direct. Mother always said that was how to speak to bring half-truths to light. Some people suffered embarrassment from their conditions and used allegory, metaphor, or outright lies to explain their maladies.

It was annoying enough when they did it, and all it would cost me was a few hours of time and some reagents I could charge them for. Now, when it could see me banished from Liúwáng ships and my family without the income I sent home, it infuriated me. "I can't help if I don't know what's going on."

Yunru's denials passed through his lips like a breath of stale air, growing more desperate with each moment. The serene façade he'd exuded earlier and every other time I'd seen him crumpled as his English fled and the words were replaced with spurts of Mandarin.

Finally, he said something with the weight of a curse and collapsed back into his seat. One leg curled awkwardly beneath him, as if he had been on the verge of falling to his knees when he went down. The intimidating person I'd tiptoed around since I joined the crew was falling apart.

He really wasn't much older than me.

"It's . . ." He sighed. "It's not my story to tell." His head sank into his hands, and he took a deep breath. "Please, just take me at my word."

Belatedly, I wondered if I should've made that tea, after all. He looked like he could use something calming. "I won't help you hide this without a good reason. I can't take that risk, not when I have people depending on me back home."

Sophia would never get into the academy without my wages. She'd be stuck on an island like St. Bernard, a hedge witch or alchemist without the skills to fly on her own and as exiled from the Liúwáng as I would be. As our father had been. A vicious cycled repeated onto another generation of innocents.

"Yunru," I said in a low voice. I could refuse a patient. I'd be damning myself if I did in this instance, but it could be done. Fan Ju was as skilled an alchemist as I; she could manage with access to my supplies, but the fact remained that a second pair of hands would do more than an endless stock of herbs. I wanted to help, but I wasn't sure I could without knowing more. "Please."

Distantly, the ship's bell called the hour, and I waited.

"Her sister might not be dead."

I blinked. Then I blinked again. A third blink finally convinced me that I was awake and this wasn't some perverse dream.

"What?" I croaked.

His hands shook and he took a deep breath. "She might not be dead. Fan Ju says she found messages in a code only she and her sister knew."

"You're lying." He had to be. There was no way someone would be stupid enough to kidnap a Liúwáng engineer and still allow them to get a message out. It was suicide to even touch a member of a Liúwáng clan, let alone harm them. Fan Ju must be imagining things in her grief, it was the only thing that made sense.

He shot a glare at me and sat up. His hands still shook, but there was a fire in his eyes now. "I would never."

"Then why would she need to hide whatever proof she has about her sister's survival? It doesn't make sense. She would've told her mother and the Liúwáng—"

"She told her mother, and her mother dismissed it as a fantasy," he said bitterly. His hands shook in his robes. "It was one of the reasons Fan Ju was placed under that spell.

Her mother worried she'd lost her sense to her grief."

"Do you have proof?" I asked hoarsely. I swallowed, but it did nothing to soothe an ache that suddenly seemed to suck the water from every part of me.

I hadn't expected this. Perhaps a revelation that Fan Ju and Yunru weren't actually married or that they'd stolen something from the clan, but not this.

He nodded. "She saw the messages in ads for Liúwáng engineers in a Dutch newspaper. She only happened to find the first one, but she recognized the code as soon as she saw it and found others soon after."

That . . . that could be proof. It could also be the desperate wishes of a grieving sister.

"But you said she fell overboard. The other engineer confirmed it. Would you doubt your own people?" The only people who suffered more for crossing the Liúwáng than mainlanders and islanders were Liúwáng who betrayed their people. It was not a fate easily faced if one wanted to live.

Yunru nodded. "That was what I believed. It took months before she could convince me to trust her in this, but I trust her now as I ask you to trust us."

By the isles, this just kept getting worse. I turned fully to face the table and sank my head into my hands, sparing a passing moment to confirm that the door was closed so none of the crew could overhear.

Yunru caught my arm, and I lifted my head to face him. He'd half risen from his chair, his face the very image of pleading, and for the first time, I truly saw him.

He was strong and stern. A capable engineer, devoted to his wife and his work, and a serious soul.

He was also very young. The last spots of youth still lingered on his face, and his body exuded the gawkiness that lingered around young men until they reached their midtwenties.

He was someone caught between the traditions of his people and his beloved wife's one chance at healing better than any a spell or potion could grant her.

He was someone as alone as I sometimes felt, only without the benefit of easy access to the rest of the crew. We were of age, and the burdens that weighed us down were equally heavy.

"Please," he whispered. "Please help my wife. Even if this ends poorly, I swear by my gods and yours that no blame will fall on you or the rest of the crew."

I hesitated, but my decision was already made.

"There's no need," I whispered, curling my hands in my pockets. "If my sisters were in that situation, I'd do whatever it took to save them."

His eyes brightened and he pulled back. "Then?"

"I'll help you." I frowned. "But she needs to come back here and give me a full rundown of those spells so I don't accidentally   trigger   them."

Interlude 2

It didn't get easier after I learned the truth of Fan Ju's pregnancy. We needed to keep it from the rest of the crew—all of whom had just as much cause to fear the Liúwáng's wrath as any sailor and were numerous enough to force Captain Proulx to turn the ship around—while keeping her healthy enough to fulfill her duties. It was a hard balance to strike, especially as Yunru began assuming some of her smaller duties.

I still remember the utter silence that fell the first time he entered the galley to fetch their dinner instead of Fan Ju. He'd wavered with a hesitance I now recognize as his unfamiliarity with non-Liúwáng cultures, as this was only his third year outside of China, but back then, it felt like utter disregard for who we were.

But eventually, even that fell into the background. My appointments with Fan Ju became commonplace, and my lessons with the crew gradually decreased as I met or exceeded their expectations. I, for once, found myself with free time I hadn't had since before I started my apprenticeship. A sailor and alchemist I might be, but everyone in the crew knew where my focus was supposed to lie.

Still, there were only so many times I could reorganize my reagents and potions that I could brew before I ran out of space, attention, and care.

This was when Fan Ju approached me with an offer to teach me the Liúwáng dialect of Mandarin in exchange for my secrecy.

Chapter 5

My days passed in a blur. In the mornings, I met with Fan Ju and discussed the spells binding her in as specific terms as we both understood while we prepared medicines. In the afternoons, I ran the rigging and the griffin's nest, making sure the runes were still intact and nothing had torn the sails or ropes while dodging the griffins themselves. My evenings were spent with Hakim and Kit, running weather rituals and casting what tracking spells Hakim and I had the energy for while using Kit as a conduit so his innate magic could strengthen our abilities. The Seven Brothers came closer each day, our progress bolstered by a strong western wind that chased us across the skies.

My lessons came to a stop, much to the despair of the crewmembers who found my struggles entertaining. Captain Proulx said I'd mastered what knowledge I'd need as a sailor and my time was better spent on more profitable ventures for the crew.

I wasn't certain I agreed, but I didn't argue. I barely had the time to eat or study, let alone patch up the myriad of smaller injuries that plagued a crew such as ours. When the last bell rang, I collapsed into my hammock and slept until the dawn came and my trials began anew.

One such morning, roughly three weeks after we set out, I woke to the morning bell and an unusual rush. The members of the third shift and first shift clustered together, their hurried muttering filling the ship's underbelly.

Cook rushed by as I settled my feet on the ground, a sack of potatoes thrown over his shoulder. "Up and at it, lad," he called, tossing me half a loaf of bread. "Sails on the horizon. Captain wants everyone on deck."

My heart thumped, and I shoved my feet in my boots. "Sails? Do we know the flag?" But the galley doors swung shut, and Cook was gone. I followed the rush to the deck—some rubbing the sleep from their eyes and others looking despairingly at the hammocks behind us—and ate my bread in hurried bites. My stomach grumbled, and I swallowed the last of my breakfast as I scanned the horizon, searching for the gleam of white that brought all of us up here.

"South by southwest," whispered a soft feminine voice right into my ear.

I nearly jumped out of my skin, and Alice burst into laughter. "Could you not do that?" I snapped, rubbing my chest to calm my rapidly beating heart. "It's too early to be creeping up on me."

She smiled and punched my shoulder. A breeze caught her loose hair and ruffled her dark green blouse. Out of port or when not gathering information, she favored practical dress over the more sultry or fashionable outfits she wore when gathering information from folks too drunk and stupid to know better than to think the pretty woman talking to them was actually interested in them. These clothes were better for climbing over the rigging, she had said, and not as well suited for pushing past drunken taverngoers. "I can't help it, you're too easy to scare."

I muttered foul words under my breath and raised my eyes to the south. When I squinted, I could just make out a dark blob on the horizon, nearly hidden by the clouds.

"Do we know the flag?" I asked, turning back to Alice.

"No one's told me yet."

Alice hummed and gathered her bright blond hair back into a thick braid. "Aye, although I doubt you would. The captain debated not stopping when we saw it, but she doesn't want to make enemies just yet."

I nodded and squinted again into the distance. The lookout's telescope would've been useful, but only the lookout was allowed to hold it.

The sky was a large place, and it wasn't common to run across another ship when you were off the popular trading routes. Etiquette required ships stop to exchange information and water, herbs, or food. That is, unless they were a plague ship or a known pirate. Those were given a wide berth.

The other sailors had dispersed. Those on the first shift hauled in the sails and slowed our progress so the other ship had time to catch up while third shift prepared the plank and lifelines. Considering how close we planned to be, the griffins might not see a sailor fall, and it paid to be prepared.

"No one we like, then? Are they English?"

Alice shook her head and stepped in front of me so as to use my relative bulk to block the wind. "No, worse. They're unlanded."

My jaw dropped, and my head whipped back toward the slowly growing blob on the horizon, the edges of their sails just becoming clear. "Pirates proper, then?" Excited thrummed through my chest, and I briefly considered the benefits of finding the lookout to steal the telescope, after all. "Or just unlanded?"

The *Vulturnus* was a privateering ship that flew under letters of marque from the French government—a right won by virtue of the captain's French father—and spent more time on legitimate trade and transportation than our seabound compatriots might, who favored battle and violence over commerce. In fact, apart from a few contractual obligations to transport French mail and dignitaries if asked, we had few responsibilities associated with the title, and those were a worthy exchange for financial help with maintaining the ship.

Unlanded ships, however, flew under no one's command but their own. They were dangerous. Smugglers, kidnappers, marauders, and thieves for hire.

Or at least, that was what we were supposed to think of them. We were all of those things, too, only we had a little piece of paper that said someone somewhere on a throne miles below and away from us approved of what we were doing.

"Unlanded as far as the lookout could tell, but the captain doesn't like them." Her grin became positively wolfish, and her voice dropped low enough, I had to bend down to hear. "It's the *Seabane*."

A chill swept through me, and I made a gesture to ward off the evil eye. "The *Seabane*? For certain? But they don't work in this hemisphere, they—"

"Have apparently come back north." She wiggled her eyebrows and clapped her hands. "Imagine the size of their commission. There's no way they'd take the risk of coming back without earning enough money to drag Fortitude down from the clouds."

I whistled and forced back a shudder.

The co-captains of the *Seabane*, twin brothers as different physically as they were alike in bloody efficiency, were two of the most ferocious pirates to have sailed the sky in a half century. They'd raided dozens of islands over the years and sent more navy vessels plummeting to a watery death than most sailors would see in their lifetimes. Their fleet had numbered in the hundreds before the combined effort of the English, French, and Dutch aerial navies had driven them away. Pirates they might be, but they were on a different level to be certain, one matched only by legends like Zheng Yi Sao, who'd convinced her government to spare criminal engineers and organized them into the Liúwáng, or the mighty Blackbeard, who struck terror into merchants all around the world.

"Bardsley!" the captain's voice rang over the deck like the thunderous clang of a bell. "Prepare your potions, I want this exchange done swiftly."

"Aye, aye," I yelled back. I nodded at Alice, who waved before heading to the wheel, and made my way below deck as Captain Proulx bellowed orders to the rest of the crew.

***

I barely managed to return to the upper deck, a crate of potions nestled in straw in hand, before the *Seabane* caught up with us. Captain Proulx waited before the plank, her features set in a deep scowl, with Hakim and Kit at her side.

"Is all prepared, Mr. Bardsley?" Hakim asked. He frowned at the box in my arms. "How much did you pack? We can't risk running short."

If I were five years younger, I'd have rolled my eyes. As such, I was well into my twenties and understood his concern. "A half dozen healing potions, three for infection, and two bottles of iron's breath to ward off pixies, sir." Less than a third of my stock, and all of them closer to expiring than I liked to keep on hand. My small amount of innate magic might allow me to manipulate some of the magic in my reagents, but time still took its due, and the last thing I wanted was to give Fan Ju or one of the other crewmembers a waning potion.

I didn't feel guilty about giving my weaker potions to another crew. A ship like the *Seabane* would surely have an alchemist or hedge witch with enough skill to bolster even my weakest potions to levels I could only dream about.

Hakim nodded. He cast a wary eye toward the *Seabane* and rested his hand on the hilt of his sabre. "Good. We don't want this to take any longer than necessary."

The *Seabane* was a ship like none I'd ever seen. Her dark blue sails spread around the ship like a flower, and her bow was carved to resemble a mighty dragon. The rumors said she'd been a British admiral's pet project, a beauty uniquely meant for aerial combat and flown through a combination of European runes and Liúwáng engineering, before the Keats twins stole her from under their watch. Each line, each seam was shaped precisely to cut through the air like a hot knife through butter. At least a dozen crewmembers clambered through the rigging, and a dozen more waited on deck, watching the proceedings like a cat watched a mouse. And in front of them, flanked by a massive red-haired woman and a wiry figure in a gray apron, were two men whose eyes were supposed to blaze like fire.

Captain Proulx grunted as the first of the mooring lines were tossed, and the *Seabane* and the *Vulturnus* were tied together. "Let's get this over with. The sooner we leave the Keats brothers behind us, the better." The plank dropped with a thunderous crash, and Captain Proulx hardly waited for it to be fastened before she moved, Hakim and Kit at her heels, and me a few steps behind.

I swallowed and gripped the box tighter. My breakfast sat heavily in my stomach and roiled in a way that had nothing to do with the spinning of two ships caught in the air. It did not escape my notice that Kit had added a sword to the daggers he habitually kept at his belt. The small knife I used for chopping reagents felt woefully inadequate.

The Keats brothers, Jacob and Robert, waited for us on

the other side.

Jacob Keats was everything that could be expected of a pirate. He was a giant of a man, all sharp edges and hard angles, head and shoulders taller than even Hakim and broad enough to make Cook look slender. Although clean-shaven, his graying black hair ran wild, as thick as a bear pelt. Tattoos covered his bare arms and what I could see of his chest. A pair of matching pistols hung from his belt, but he didn't touch them. His face was unreadable, the fire in his eyes briefly tamped down, but they lingered covetously on the box in my arms.

Robert Keats, on the other hand, looked like a merchant. His clothing was fine, a collection of lace and silk that would make half the ladies back home green with envy, and his thick, red beard would've done the same to most of the men. Whatever muscle he possessed was hidden underneath his finery. He smiled broadly at Captain Proulx and stepped forward with open arms, pleasantries spilling from his lips.

As surreptitiously as I could, I glanced between the two brothers, my mind not quite wanting to follow where rumor had led me.

But looks were deceiving, I reminded myself. Jacob was not the one who'd ordered a half dozen ships scuttled before their crews abandoned them. Robert's softness hid the steel underneath. He was every bit as ruthless as his brother where it really counted.

"Welcome to the *Seabane*," Robert said, spreading his silk-covered arms wide, his English tinted with just the slightest French lilt. "Captain Proulx, *mon amie*, it is a pleasure to see you again." His lips pulled back in a smile that was too wide to be genuine.

Captain Proulx nodded. "And you, Captain Robert, Captain Jacob."

Jacob grunted. His eyes never left me, and I felt myself flush under the weight of his gaze.

I tore my eyes away and focused deliberately on Captain Proulx and Captain Robert, who nodded and beckoned for those standing behind him to step forward. "Allow me to introduce Ms. Grace O'Malley, our first mate, and Alfred Smith, our quartermaster. They've got a better understanding of what we're running short of than I do, unfortunately."

A massive redhead and a scrawny gray-haired man stepped forward. Ms. O'Malley was the redheaded woman I'd seen earlier, and up close, she was even bigger than I'd thought. She'd have been the tallest person I'd ever met if it weren't for the presence of Captain Jacob, who towered over her by at least three inches. Mr. Smith, in comparison, was a tiny scrap of a man in a gray apron who lingered in her shadow, a thick book clutched in his arms.

Robert's smile grew wider still but failed to reach his eyes. "Captain Proulx," he purred, holding a hand out as if she were a dainty mainland princess waiting to be carried off, "perhaps we could adjourn to the stateroom while our crews negotiate. We recently acquired an excellent brandy."

Captain Proulx raised an eyebrow and opened her mouth, but before she could answer, Captain Jacob spoke.

"Robert." His voice was deceptively quiet. No louder than a whisper or perhaps a murmur, but it still cut across the deck like he'd shouted. "We are not here for their company. Let us complete our business and be on our way."

Robert's lips turned down in a pout, and then he released an explosive sigh. "Brother, you are so cruel to me."

Jacob's eyebrow rose higher.

A silent conversation passed between the brothers before Robert let out another sigh. "Very well," he said, turning back to Captain Proulx with exaggerated sadness on his face. "We shall have to have the pleasure of your company on another night, perhaps after our business is completed."

Captain Proulx's face had fallen back into careful neutrality, and she nodded. "Of course." She gestured toward me. "My alchemist has prepared a collection of potions we can afford to lose. My husband will speak with Mr. Smith about the finer details."

**

The trade went quickly once Robert was persuaded to step back and let his crew handle the transaction.

Mr. Smith took all the potions offered and weaseled three bags of reagents off me as well. Apparently their alchemist had taken ill and couldn't leave his bed. The potions and reagents would tide them over until either the alchemist recovered or his apprentice could go ashore to find more reagents.

I stayed quiet during the negotiations, for the most part. Occasionally, Mr. Smith would ask a question about the reagents and the potions, but there were only so many times he could ask for clarity before Hakim shut him down. We ended up with an extra barrel of water, two sacks of potatoes, and a hundred feet of rope in exchange for our goods while Kit and Ms. O'Malley glared daggers at each other. Kit's evil eye was quite impressive for someone who had to crane his neck back to even look his opponent in the face.

All in all, for an hour or two in the beating sun, we hadn't come out too badly. At least, not from my perspective. The others felt otherwise.

Captain Proulx kept her face diplomatically blank until

we'd cast off and the *Seabane* and her crew were away. Once they were gone, she sighed explosively and rubbed her temples.

"All right, back to your duties," she muttered. "Mr. Bardsley, please fetch something for a headache and then meet us in the stateroom. Alice will know to find us there. We'll need to discuss this."

Hakim and Kit nodded grimly and marched off. Kit went to the wheel to account for the time and space we'd drifted while tied to the *Seabane*, and Hakim went to the hold to account for our gains and losses.

In no time at all, I was alone on the deck. Captain Proulx had already strode off, her hat pulled low over her eyes. The wind tugged at her coat and braids, but the bite didn't seem to bother her at all.

It was different in my case. A sharp wind caught my clothes, bringing an unseasonable chill and the distant smell of rain with it. Shivering, I hurried after Captain Proulx.

***

"You have a talent for languages," Yunru called from behind a curtain on the far side of the cabin.

I shrugged despite knowing he couldn't see me. "I speak Greek, French, Latin, German, and English fluently already. Mandarin is a challenge, but so is every language in its own way."

Fan Ju chuckled as she packed away the chalk and slate that she used for vocabulary. "But it is not an easy tongue, especially for many of your kin. Even some of the Liúwáng born outside our homeland and raised on the Flying Isles struggle with the finer points."

It was harsh but fair. Unfortunately for most of my heritage, the mainlander nobility had a disregard for cultures outside their borders, and the lower classes had few opportunities to study on their own.

"It is all by the good graces of my teachers," I said awkwardly. I should've known better than to take them up on their offer to teach me, but anyone who spoke Mandarin—and especially the Liúwáng dialect—was worth their weight in gold. Besides, it would've been more suspicious if I'd turned them down, or so I told the little voice in the back of my mind. They, too, knew the value of their tongue for a merchant. Even if I never worked on a ship again after this voyage, hell, even if I were exiled, the knowledge I gained would make my translating services invaluable.

So I had swallowed my fears and accepted their invitation. Normally these lessons took place after my shift above deck finished, but our encounter with the *Seabane* had thrown everything off schedule. By the time I'd give the captain her headache remedy, chased down a proper meal, and finished my duties, the sun was edging close to the horizon.

Fan Ju had grabbed my arm before I could retreat to my storeroom, unwilling to miss even a single day's worth of learning.

The lessons took place inside their quarters, where few others were allowed to go. This had the dual benefit of providing access to learning materials and a hidden place for me to examine Fan Ju and exchange potions for whatever reagents she wished me to use in the future. In the time since we departed Fortitude, she'd taken to minimizing the time she spent outside her quarters. A slighter woman would've needed to hide herself away a month ago, but as it was, she wouldn't be able to hide her condition for much longer.

She and Yunru would need to switch tasks on the way back, assuming she still wished to hide her pregnancy from the rest of the crew. He would handle their interactions with the crew, and she would take the lion's share of managing the ship. Once we returned to Fortitude, they would speak with Fan Ju's mother, and the issue would leave my hands.

The crew was only vaguely polite in their prodding questions about what lay beyond the door to the engineers' compartment. Only Captain Proulx and Cook had ever been invited inside before now, and wise folks left those two alone lest they found themselves in the crow's nest overnight and on an empty stomach. Even Hakim had never been allowed inside.

The fact that I, a simple alchemist, was called in daily set most tongues wagging. Those tongues, in turn, took advantage of my guild oath to treat them no matter how much they annoyed me to badger me with an unending number of questions.

"A teacher is only as good as their student." Fan Ju smiled and set a steaming pot on the short table where we held our lessons. She reclined on the cushion opposite me and set out three delicate porcelain cups. "And you are more willing to listen to scolding than some among us."

Yunru said something in Mandarin too quick for my limited vocabulary to catch, and Fan Ju laughed. She returned the commentary in kind, and Yunru accepted it with some mild grumbling.

"Was Yunru not a good student?" I asked before I could think better of it.

"Ha! He was a menace." Fan Ju poured the tea, giggling all the while. She held a teacup near the gap in the curtain and smiled at me. "There was a reason he came to my family when he became Liúwáng. None of the others would have him. He was all bluster and outrage, fighting everyone who tried to help, until my mother took him in

90

hand."

"I was not that bad," Yunru called, sticking his hand out to take the mug without making a gap larger than his hand in the heavy cloth dividing us.

"You were, even my mother—" A loud clang came from above deck, and we both paused, Fan Ju halfway through lifting her cup to her mouth, and me poring over my notes. "Is that—?"

The bell rang again and I jolted to my feet. Once could've been an hour marker, twice could've been a shift change, but any more . . .

The bell rang for a third time and then didn't stop. I swore under my breath and ran out, throwing an apology over my shoulder. I burst into the hall and joined the hoard racing up to the deck.

Three or more was an emergency. The only ones who weren't required to report for duty were Cook and the engineers.

We emerged into the fading light darkened further still by black clouds looming over the horizon. The air crackled and thrummed with electricity, and I swallowed.

"All hands to your squall stations," Captain Proulx roared from her place by the helmsman's side. "Prepare for the storm—"

Thunder roared, drowning out the last of her words, but we didn't need them to know our duties. We were below the cloudline, and that was an exceptionally bad place to be during a squall.

Once I tied my lifeline around my waist, I raced up the rigging with the others of the first shift. We would prepare the sails and ropes for the squall while the others cleared the deck and readied the lightning protection. The thunder cracked, boomed, and roared as the wind picked up until even the loudest shout was whisked away before it had even been given voice.

The griffins' cries were the only thing to echo louder than the storm, their place in the nest long since abandoned as they swooped around the ship. Their keepers stood on the edge of the deck, silent whistles in hand, to alert their charges to any crew blown overboard.

The first lightning bolt struck as I made my way down the rigging. For a heartbeat, the sky was brighter than the sun before the whole ship shook with the force of the blow. A piercing squeal split the air, and the heavens opened. Ropes and wood alike grew slick in the onslaught, and I prayed the others would keep their footings as I drew closer to the deck.

If we were exceptionally lucky, the most I would have to deal with once this was all through were bruises and cuts. If we weren't, someone would break a limb, and I didn't want to use more potions than I had to. Weak as they were, the ones we'd traded to the *Seabane* would've gone a long way toward soothing minor injuries, and I hadn't had time to replenish them.

My mind was briefly put at ease when I reached the ground, but it wasn't to last.

"Edward, we need you below," Hakim yelled, his voice barely audible over the screaming of the wind. "Andyrs is waiting, she—"

But the thunder drowned him out, and I didn't wait for clarity. Andyrs was on third shift, and they'd been assigned to the lightning protection. I'd seen that go wrong before.

The sudden shift from pouring rain and howling winds to the relative silence of below deck—broken only by the soft moaning and swearing of my patient—was jarring, but I put it out of my mind.

Andyrs, a middle-aged Finnish woman, and Jinhai, a Chinese man whom I'd shared a number of meals with, were waiting for me, water pooling underneath them. Jinhai helped me get Andyrs, whose lanky frame belied how heavy she was, onto my table, muttered a quick explanation for her injuries, and then left me to my work.

Andyr's injuries were severe. A poorly timed slip had sent her tumbling onto the lightning rod just when the lightning struck, and only the quick thinking of the fire brigade had kept her from going up in flames. Her hands were a mess, her fingers melted and fused together, and the lightning left scars in its own image across the left half of her body.

I swore violently and set to work, pulling potions and salves free of their places.

It didn't end there. After the wind picked up, a handful of others came in trailing broken lifelines behind them and blood dripping from the talon marks on their shoulders. After that came a man knocked senseless by a stumble down the stairs. For nearly an hour I worked without stopping. The few of those healthy enough to move but not healthy enough to go above deck were set to work minding the injured in the hold.

I nearly missed it. During a lull, a pause in the flow of wounded, I glanced out the window at the same time as a bolt of lightning. My ears ached from the screaming and the constant thunder, but I saw it. A faint outline in the clouds, with sails spread around it like a deathly halo. Electricity had crackled through the cloth, and I nearly yelled for someone to alert the captain to a ship in danger, but there was no spark of flame. The sails hardly seemed to move in the stiff breeze.

I often cursed myself for not reporting this, but Andyrs chose that moment to awaken, and her screams drove the image from my mind.

Chapter 6

Storms followed us the entire way to the Seven Brothers. Thankfully, there were no injuries as bad as the first, but those were bad enough. Andyrs was stuck on a cot in my storeroom for three days before I dubbed her healed enough to resume light duties, and Jinhai joined her as often as his duties would allow. My limbs shook with exhaustion, both magical and benign. Every waking moment was spent restocking my potion supply and using what little energy I had left for weather-predicting spells that weren't predicting the squalls like they should have.

Fan Ju joined me when she could. Large robes hid her growing belly whenever she helped me with the wounded or chanced an appointment in my storeroom. Our lessons in Mandarin continued in the brief moments I had time to breathe, but I hadn't been back to their cabin since the first storm.

The day the Seven Brothers finally appeared on the horizon, the crew let out a ragged cheer. They were as exhausted as I was. Everyone had been pulling double shifts, and not even the most tantalizing of Cook's meals or anything I could add to the coffee could make up for lost sleep and long hours. Actually reaching our goal meant there was a chance for rest in our future.

The largest of the Seven Brothers had a sizable port town named Leyden. It was mostly inhabited by Dutch immigrants—the descendants of the original merchants who'd founded the town and the servants they'd brought along to make their journeys more comfortable—and laborers hired to actually build everything alongside small enclaves of fae folk that handled griffon breeding and specialized runecraft. It wasn't as impressive as Fortitude, but it didn't need to be. Its shipyards were a thing of beauty, putting out Liúwáng- and mage-flown ships alike in under eighteen months, and its markets specialized in luxury goods. It was also mostly owned by the Van der Bergs, and they guarded their belongings fiercely.

We didn't land on the largest island despite the damage our ship had sustained since the storms started. Mostly because the damage was more irritating than it was disabling, but also because it was better to keep a low profile when planning to rob someone. Avoiding a long drop and a sudden stop was high on all our priority lists.

It was fortunate then that the smallest of these islands had enough of a waterline to make landfall and was also far enough away from the main island that we could hide the *Vulturnus* with relative ease.

While the majority of the crew made repairs, Alice and three of the sneakier crewmembers (Kit and Cook noticeably not among them, to their chagrin) would go onto the largest island for reconnaissance. When they returned, we would finalize our plans for actually recovering the master's stolen goods.

Or at least this was our plan. It didn't go that smoothly in practice.

The reconnaissance should've been a matter of hours, a half day at most, but we'd finished the biggest repairs and the sun had long since set by the time the lookout spotted them rowing back.

Captain Proulx ordered them into her cabin and emerged two hours later wearing a look that could've curdled milk.

Despite the late hour, she called myself, Kit, and Cook

to the meeting, and we were treated to a rundown of what Alice's team had discovered.

The Van der Bergs had spent the last few years building up Leyden's defenses, and the wealthier part of an already prosperous town had become a veritable fortress. Cannons lined the walls, and the armories could've outlasted a mainland invasion.

Beyond that, there was a regular standing guard, three hundred strong and financed entirely by the Van der Bergs. Their patrols were regular and thorough, and the last unfortunate soul to attempt bribery still hung from the gibbet with the one who'd accepted right beside him with a bag of gold around what was left of her neck.

The Van der Bergs paid well indeed to ensure loyalty. Their punishments for betraying their generosity ensured their investments paid off.

Their precautions put us in a tight spot.

We obviously couldn't raid them. No matter how skilled the crew, a five-cannon ship with fewer than fifty crewmembers couldn't hope to outfight the guard, outrun the frigates looking to cash in on the Van der Bergs' standing bounty on pirates, and still have an intact vessel to get home.

So we opted for stealth instead. Riskier, perhaps, but less likely to result in premature hanging.

Despite our wishes otherwise, we would need to dock at Leyden. Alice and Kit would go ashore in costume as a wealthy French merchant and her husband who'd hired the ship, captain, and crew rather than build their own. It'd be expensive, but hopefully we'd be able to offload the goods at Fortitude when everything was said and done. The alibi for our presence thus established in such a way as to keep the more recognizable members of the crew out of sight—namely Captain Proulx, Hakim, and Cook, who'd apparently worked on board a number of Dutch vessels over the years and fostered a love of Scottish whisky in many of his employers—the next stage of our plan could begin.

Under the influence of a notice-me-not spell—which I would cast with Cook providing the power to maintain it—a select team would slip onshore the following night. Through methods I wasn't privy to, they would slip inside the Van der Bergs' keep. Over three days, they would observe the routine, locate the chest the master swore his goods would still be inside, and then strike.

Captain Proulx planned to hide the master's chest among the goods Alice and Kit acquired, then leave with the tide and vague promises to return once we'd emptied our hold.

Cook didn't like it. He didn't like any plan that saw Kit and Alice leave his side. We didn't have a choice though. Of the entire crew, only Alice, Captain Proulx, and myself had the background knowledge necessary to come off as a merchant, and Captain Proulx didn't want to risk her face becoming known in the days before the Van der Bergs were robbed.

Despite Cook's concerns, it was a good plan as far as I could tell. My own part was small but essential, and with luck and skill, it should work.

***

"Any news?" Cook asked as soon as he shoved his way through my door. He set the tray with my meal on the ground next to me and crouched at my side. The elaborate circle I'd drawn on the ground thrummed with energy at his approach, and I gently pushed him back before his innate magic overloaded the spellwork.

Maintaining this spellwork was difficult enough without the conduit causing problems. As small as this part might be, it was still essential to the plan, and more importantly, it was my job to do it.

"None of the wards have been triggered, which means they haven't been found yet." Notice-me-not was a notoriously finicky spell, one I normally wouldn't have been able to produce on my own. It needed a constant flow of innate magic and attention to hold its power, and I could only provide one of those things.

That being said, there were wondrous things one could do with the right runes and the right reagents. Sharing magical power was one small part of that, but still one that alchemists like myself had been using for ages.

Cook had volunteered the surprisingly deep wells of innate magic that thrummed through his veins for this endeavor. Hakim and I drew runes on my body and his to give me greater control over his power than standard conduit runes could manage, which was the one way I could cast a spell of this caliber. The small amount of innate magic in my body was just enough to maintain the link between Cook and me, provided his innate magic didn't rebel against being used like this.

I'd barely slept in two days, but all my work was paying off. The power stayed consistent, and the wards hadn't so much as flickered. We might yet pull this off.

"Good." Cook grunted and squinted at the runes. "Let me know if anything changes. I have the lads preparing something fun just in case things go wrong."

"Should I be concerned?" Perhaps I should be. Cook was usually a voice of reason in the crew, but I'd heard enough stories about his previous voyages to be cautious when he said he had a plan.

Shifting into a seated position, he hummed noncommittally. "Just a small thing. I've rigged my still to blow the dock. With luck, it'll just be a waste of product, but I'd rather have it set to go than not."

It would also effectively prevent the Van der Bergs from launching any ships while they dealt with the flaming docks alongside the damage to their ships. A decent, if dangerous, way to distract the Van der Bergs, provided we could get far enough away before it blew.

I decided I didn't want to know more and picked at my food and coffee. In a few hours, the crew inside the keep would sneak out, and then I could rest. I just needed to make it that long.

Cook hadn't left yet, but he wasn't making noise, so I paid him no mind as I carefully ate. Both the people who'd received his bracelets were gone. I wasn't sure what protections or spells had been cast on them, but I could feel the gentle siphon of energy that fueled them. As long as Cook kept quiet, I wouldn't begrudge him whatever he needed to do to reassure himself of Kit and Alice's safety.

The hours crept by like a becalmed sea. The waves gently rocked the ship, which creaked and groaned around us. The docks' hawkers closed their stalls and left as the workday drew to a close. Cook stayed on the far side of the circle. His eyes never lifted from its softly glowing edges as he tapped a steady rhythm on his upper arms.

When the sun dipped below the horizon and the light of the circle became the only thing keeping my storeroom from plunging into total darkness, Cook jerked up.

"That can't be . . ." he whispered under his breath, staring out the window behind me. "It's too public here." His face dropped into a heavy scowl, and he shoved himself to his feet. "Hold on, lad, I'll be right back."

In my exhaustion, I nearly turned to see what had drawn his attention, but caught myself at the last moment. Another hour yet before I could look away. The wards needed constant attention, especially when I wasn't the one providing the magic. The others should be out of the keep by now, but we'd all agreed it was better to be safe about it.

Still, the creak of steps on the deck above lingered with the distant hum of voices I couldn't place. Cook's familiar brogue filtered down, each word muffled by the hum between my ears and the distance between us. I didn't recognize the other voices, but I didn't care to try.

But even that distraction cost me. The circle flickered on and off, the edges crackling and breaking, and it took me a handful of seconds we didn't have to reinforce it. I threw myself forward, slammed my shaking hands down, and pulled as much energy as I dared from Cook.

The circle fought back. It crackled and thrummed beneath me, responding sluggishly to my efforts to reinforce it. My eyes slid shut, and I swore under my breath. Without the distraction of sight, I could see clearer than before. The circle struggled against an unseen foe, a darkness that tugged at the edges, willing the circle to split and shatter. I poured more energy inside, tracing the runes with my mind's eye, willing them to stay whole and secure.

The darkness tangled around my thoughts, tearing at the threads connecting me to Cook and the circle. I pushed back at it, reinforcing the magic thrumming through the circle and sending off a splinter to lash at the interloper.

I don't know how long we fought. All my attention was consumed by the battle and the overarching panic about what it meant for those still in Leyden. If the circle broke now, they'd be completely exposed. We couldn't get caught now. We needed more time—

Then without warning, the assault stopped. The circle settled, and only the thought of ruining all my hard work kept me from collapsing then and there.

I let out a ragged gasp, and my eyes shot open. My stomach roiled, and I took deep and even breaths to steady it. My thoughts ran in circles, mindlessly cataloging what had happened while my body tried to get back to something resembling equilibrium.

And all the while, one worry ran through my head: That hadn't come from Alice or the rest of her team. Someone had tried to break the circle. Someone close by.

If I'd had the breath, I'd have cursed. As it was, I struggled to maintain the circle and my consciousness. The world pitched and spun like a top, and my head felt as heavy as the ship itself.

I needed to stay awake. Hakim would know what to do. He knew more about magic circles than I did, but I needed to stay awake until he got here so I could tell him what had happened.

The pounding of footsteps echoed through the hold and came to a stop outside my door. Cook was the first in, his voice thundering through the ship like a gong.

"What happened, lad? I felt it—" He skidded to a stop, took in my haggard appearance and how my eyes refused to focus, and swore. "Did the circle break? Are the others all right?"

I shook my head, and the motion sent my world spinning. "No, it . . ." The words wouldn't come. My tongue felt thick as cotton, and I swallowed painfully. How long had it been since Cook left? How long had I been sitting here?

Captain Proulx shoved Cook aside, Hakim at her heels. "What happened?" she demanded.

Hakim came to my side and raised a waterskin to my lips. I drank greedily, the water spilling over my lips and onto my shirt. When it was emptied, I fell back, gasping for air.

"Someone tried to break the circle after Cook left," I said once I had my breath back. "I stopped them."

"Aye, and nearly killed yourself doing so," Cook muttered. He'd left me to Captain Proulx and Hakim and leaned over the circle once more. "And me too. You're lucky I was sitting when you started pulling like that."

The circle. I'd forgotten—

I threw myself off Hakim and toward the circle. To my great relief, it still thrummed with energy. Miraculously, my brief lapse in attention hadn't broken it. The energy I'd forced into it while trying to keep it intact had held it in place while I'd been distracted.

"It's still going strong, don't worry." Hakim caught my shoulder and saved me from tumbling over. "It's late enough, you can probably drop the spell . . ." He squinted oddly at the circle.

"What'd you do to my ship, Bardsley?" Captain Proulx asked, and I'd have jumped if I had the energy. She hadn't moved since barging into the storeroom, and I'd forgotten she was there.

I gestured toward the circle. If it weren't for the way my limbs trembled, I might have kept a more respectful tone, but that would've required energy. "I did my job, Captain."

She snorted. "You burned the circle into the wood."

I blinked and then squinted at the circle. The light didn't hurt my eyes after staring at it for most of the day, but it was still bright. If I looked closely, I could see the ash spreading beneath it. "I think it should wash off."

"Let the circle down," Captain Proulx ordered. "We're past the marked hour, and you're too exhausted for sense."

I let the circle down, and the sudden absence of the drain on my energy and attention was dizzying.

"Thank you, Captain," I mumbled.

She signed and massaged her forehead. "Cook, get something of substance in him. The night's not over yet. Hakim and I will deal with this."

Cook took me by the arm and half dragged me to the galley. I was too drained to do more than stumble along behind him. He nudged me toward a table, and I slumped into a bench, laying my head down for a moment's rest.

Footsteps preceded a bowl nudging my arm, and I blearily lifted my head to start eating. Cook sat across from me, a matching bowl and two chunks of bread between us.

"Eat," he ordered, ripping one of the chunks in half before dipping it into his bowl. "I won't have you collapsing from hunger."

I grunted and nibbled at my stew. It was thick and heady, with chunks of fresh beef and diced vegetables. My arms shook so badly, I struggled to hold the spoon, but after a few bites, they steadied. By the time I finished my bowl and bread—and a second, more generous portion of both—the overwhelming exhaustion had tapered down into something more manageable.

I pushed the empty bowl away and took a long drink of the flagon that had appeared midway through my meal. The ale went down smoothly, and my limbs felt loose and free.

"Glad to see your appetite wasn't hurt," Cook said with a laugh. He gestured at his bowl, which was only half-empty. "Are you done, or would you like more?"

I pondered that for a minute. I certainly could eat more, but right now my stomach felt pleasantly full, and I didn't want to push that feeling too far. After all, I still had to do this tomorrow, and facing monotonous hours of watch with an upset stomach was a step further than I wanted to go.

Mind made up, I shook my head. "No, I'm done now."

A thought occurred to me, even as I spoke. "What about you? The wards pulled a lot of energy from you. Are you all right?"

Cook shrugged. "I was sitting when the drain began. Since I wasn't the one maintaining the magic, it didn't hit me as hard. Our guests assumed I was drunk."

"But still . . ." My body ached just remembering how it felt, but with food in my belly and a chance to rest, I could think clearly now. "Do we know what happened? Whoever tried to break the circle had to have been close by."

Snorting, Cook leaned forward and rested his head on his joined hands. "The *Seabane* happened. We found out who they're working for."

My heart plunged to my stomach. The ale sat uneasily with the stew now, and I set the flagon down. "What do you mean?"

"I mean the Van der Bergs have hired them to 'provide security consultations and escort services.'" He scowled and took a swig from his flagon. Wiping his mouth on his sleeve, he continued, "They recognized the ship, and old Robert and Jacob stopped by with their stooges to check in on how we'd handled the storms. Robert wouldn't stop talking about how he had no idea we were headed here, and that he'd have warned us about the heavy storm season if only he'd known." He spat and took another deep drink. "Bullshit, in my opinion."

I nodded, my mind whirling with the implications. "So they have a mage, then?" Only someone with an incredible amount of technical skill—or enough sheer innate magical power to overload the wards—could try to break a circle like that, and the average alchemist didn't have the strength I'd felt. If it was an alchemist, then they'd be on par with the hedge witch that had cast the tracking spell on Fan Ju. The only reason I'd been able to make that circle was because Hakim's scholarly background more than made up for the gaps in my practical knowledge, and Cook's raw power was the only reason it had stayed intact. "Isn't the *Seabane* a Liúwáng-run ship? I thought they didn't like having mages on board."

Everyone knew that Liúwáng didn't like mages on their ships. Alchemists were acceptable only because our magic was contained, and we already knew how to work our craft around whatever magic was in our surroundings. Mages were more . . . vocal with their abilities, which made sense to me. Mother always said she'd never met a mage that wasn't an absolute show-off.

Cook shrugged. "That or an alchemist who ought to have been a mage. Either way, they came looking for us, and then someone sensed and tried to break your circle. If that's a coincidence, I'll give up the drink."

I let out a quiet whistle. Cook was a distrustful bastard at the best of times, but he drank more than most of the crew combined. Stopping might kill him. "Do you think—"

An explosion shook the ship, knocking over our flagons and shattering a window. Both of us leaped to our feet, dishes and spilled drink forgotten in our rush above deck.

Even as we moved, the town bells rang out their terrible song, calling all outside.

We burst onto deck into a scene from the apocalypse. The keep was in flames, and a full third was just . . . gone. Black smoke blocked out the stars, and screams filled the air.

Houses, shops, and ships alike were coated in debris. No window I could see had survived the catastrophe. Embers and sparks spread by the explosion caught the buildings they'd landed on, and already flames started to lick fresh thatching.

Cook swore and dove for the fire bucket. "The sails," he roared, "wet the sails before another powder room catches, hurry!"

It took a moment for his words to penetrate the horror that filled my senses, but eventually they got through. I threw myself into the rigging alongside five others that had followed Cook and me to the deck, and caught the bucket he threw to me, heedless of the water splashing over the sides and soaking my shirt.

We couldn't let the sails catch fire. We'd never get off the water without them, but we couldn't leave without Alice, Kit, and the others.

All around us, ships in our situation were doing the same thing, and ones that could had already begun pulling away. All that was needed to turn the harbor to ash was the wind shifting direction.

The bells had drawn the sailors from their leave, the citizens from their homes, and the merchants from their stores and stalls. The crowd of people were drawn in one of two ways: either to the keep to tend the main fire, or to the harbor to catch a ship before it left without them.

My limbs burned and shook, but each bucket was a step closer to salvation. By now, what crew had been sleeping below deck had joined the bucket chain, and mine weren't the only hands working.

Acrid smoke burned my eyes and nostrils as Hakim's and Captain Proulx's voices rose above the clamor. Cook had disappeared, but as long as the next bucket hit my hands, I couldn't be bothered to look for him. I'd climbed to the very top of the rigging, just below the griffin's nest, and by now there were fifteen souls up there with me, and the rest of the crew was below, filling anything that could be used to hold water just in case. The griffins screamed and squawked, their tethers barely winning the battle to keep them on the ship.

It was only this vantage point—and a wing to the face that nearly knocked me off the rigging—that allowed me to see Alice's distinctive blue merchant's dress in the crowd. Two of the crew who'd gone with her ran in front of her, a heavy-looking chest hanging between them, and a third figure hung over her shoulders, presumably Kit, but as they drew ever closer, I realized whomever it was wasn't nearly bulky enough to be him. Looping an arm through the rigging, I cupped both hands over my mouth and yelled to those below.

"Crew coming up dockside! Crew coming up dockside, clear my way!"

I wasn't sure what had possessed Alice to light the keep on fire, but it did serve as an excellent distraction. The guards would be too preoccupied with keeping the flames from the warehouses to notice whatever else she'd done.

Those below me parted to let me pass, and I climbed down as quickly as I could. My limbs might shake, but whomever Alice was carrying would need help, and we could spare a hand in the rigging now.

I hit the deck as Alice crested the plank, and I ran up to her. "How bad is it?"

Alice seemed eager to pass her burden on to me. "Unclear. Van der Berg had her chained to a wall. We found her in the same room as the chest." She kept looking behind her, back toward the town, as if willing something to appear. She glanced back, and the wave of anger that flowed off her could've killed a whale.

I stumbled under the added weight. It wasn't as much as I expected for someone this size. The Dutch weren't known for being forgiving, but I'd assumed they fed their prisoners at least. It was too dark for clearer details, so I went off what I could guess from my other senses. "Right. Any other injuries or should we go below deck?"

But Alice glared instead of answering, and it could've stripped fresh paint off the walls. "We were seen because the wards weakened," she finally hissed. "Whoever she is, she threatened to call for the guards if we didn't take her with us. We could've actually done this right if you'd done your job."

My stomach clenched and I swallowed. "I didn't—"

"Save it. I need to talk to the captain."

And she stormed off, something glittering in her eyes. A part of me wanted desperately to call her back, to explain, but the injured woman on my shoulder released a moan, and I remembered my place.

Captain Proulx and Hakim would explain why the wards had weakened. In the meantime, I needed to tend my   patient.   Alice would . . . She'd understand. Cook could vouch for me too. I'd done my best.

I dragged my patient through the throngs of sailors as Captain Proulx's calls changed from fire safety to getting the ship ready to launch. I hadn't seen Kit, but he must've come on board while I was talking to Alice. The captain wouldn't leave without him.

The patient groaned and muttered things in a vaguely familiar language as I moved below deck, eager to get her in place before Cook's still blew. It wouldn't be long at this point. The wind had to shift eventually, and whatever he left behind would catch like a firework. The ship thrummed with energy, like the boards and ropes of the *Vulturnus* itself couldn't wait to be away. Her eyes fluttered open when I laid her on my cot, and she let out a pitiful moan.

Using a calm and steady voice, I reassured her that she was safe and that I was a trained alchemist while I fiddled with the lamps. Healing was best done when one could see what was going on, as my mother liked to say. In what little light came through my window, all I could tell for certain was that she was human. The lamps swayed as the ship moved, the distant clanging of the bells becoming quieter with each passing second.

I chanced a glance out the window and let loose a relieved sigh to see that we'd taken flight. It was fortunate we left when we did, because no sooner had we cleared the edge of the water than the dock vanished in a blaze of fire and smoke, taking three ships with it.

I turned back to my patient and felt a knot of tension leave me to see she was sitting up. "If you can understand me, can you tell me where you're hurt? I have potions if it's serious." If it were one of the crew, I wouldn't bother with this. I had blanket approval to do whatever was necessary to keep everyone alive and as healthy as possible, no matter what it took. I did not have permission to act as I wanted with strangers, though, and this one was awake and moving.

She met my eyes, and thanks to the lamps, I got my first proper look at her. My breath caught in my chest. "You're Asian," I said stupidly. Even with the heavy bruising and the blood covering half her face, it was obvious. "Are you Liúwáng?"

If she was Liúwáng, then we had a whole host of new problems. If the Van der Bergs had imprisoned her, she'd probably done something terrible. If she wasn't . . . Well, it didn't sound like Alice had found her in the regular cells.

She blinked up at me and spat something in furious and slurred Mandarin. I didn't catch any of it.

I pulled back and swallowed. Right. There was an

injured and possibly Liúwáng woman in my storeroom. Fan Ju and Yunru would be too busy getting the ship away from the port to help, and any new injuries would be coming down here soon. I didn't have time to panic about this. *"I am* Edward Bardsley, *I am an alchemist,"* I said in halting Mandarin. My lessons hadn't been going on long, but Fan Ju had taught me the most important phrases for someone like me to know. Whomever this woman was, she still needed care, at least until we were far enough out of danger that Fan Ju and Yunru could take her in. *"Are you hurt?"*

The anger in her face turned to surprise, and she eased back onto the cot. *"You speak Mandarin?"* she demanded, her dark eyes carefully cataloging the storeroom. *"Are you with—"* She used a word I didn't know, but I could tell it wasn't polite. One didn't usually have nice things to say about people holding you captive.

"I am an alchemist with Vulturnus. *We go away."* It wasn't pretty, but it did the job. Still, most Liúwáng spoke the major trade tongues, and I'd rather avoid translation errors if I could. It'd speed things up at the very least. *"You speak English? Dutch? French?"*

My Dutch was far from fluent, but it was better than my Mandarin. Fortunately, she answered in English.

She let out an explosive sigh and lay back down, massaging her wrists. "Did we get away?"

I nodded. "We just left port."

The bells got quieter and quieter as we flew away. Leaving under cover of darkness wasn't ideal, but the farther away we were when Van der Berg realized he'd been robbed, the better.

"May I look at your injuries?" Normally, I wouldn't push her, but the situation hadn't changed. I still needed to look over the rest of Alice's group and anyone who had gotten burned before we could get away.

She shook her head and drew her arms close to her. "No," she said quickly, and then paused as if considering what to say. "It's nothing serious. That—" She repeated the phrase she said earlier. "Made sure to have me treated if his men got too rough. He paid too much for me to risk losing me to an infection because his guards wanted to have some fun."

Ah. Perhaps I should grab Fan Ju, after all. The last thing I wanted was to make a bad situation worse.

"Well, there are healing potions in the lower cabinet and bandages on the shelf. I've labeled everything in English, French, and Mandarin, so let me know if you can't find anything. I'll knock before I come in again, all right?"

The bells had gotten louder again, far louder than they should be. I glanced out the window to see if we'd doubled back. But no, those were . . . those were coming from the ship.

"I've got to go. If you can walk, the engineers' quarters are on the other side of the hold."

I ran out and above deck, praying I heard wrong.

Thunder cracked and roared when I emerged, and rain beat on my face. The wind picked up, blowing and tearing at anything not tied down. The sky lit up with glorious bangs and crashes every few seconds, and I swore violently. The whole ship shook as lightning hit our rod, and it was then that I realized what was happening.

In the heartbeat between the lightning lighting up the sky and it fading again, I saw it. A ship following us. One with wide sails that spread out around the ship like a deadly flower. The lightning danced up and down them, along ropes and rigging, lighting up runes and spellwork.

This wasn't a storm. We were under attack.

Chapter 7

"Sails off the port quarter," I shouted, scrambling for the upper deck. I pointed frantically toward where I'd seen the *Seabane.* "Captain, we're under attack, it's the *Seabane!*"

I tore up to Hakim, who was wrestling the wheel into submission with the helmsman, and skidded to a stop on the wet deck. "Sir, we're under attack——" Even as I spoke, the lightning cracked again, deafening thunder on its heels. It was too close. They'd brought the storm up out of nowhere, and if we weren't quick, it would bring us down. Bloody hell, they must've been following us all the way to the Seven Brothers. How had they known we were headed there?

"A weather mage," Hakim said hoarsely. He swore violently, leaving the helmsman to take the wheel for himself. "Battle stations," he roared, spittle flying from his mouth as he rang the alarm bell furiously. "All free hands to battle stations."

I turned back around, seeking anything I could do. I ought to go back below deck, to my storeroom to prepare for any injuries, but I didn't dare. The Keats brothers had persuaded their engineer to allow a mage on board, and we had no way of knowing what they could do.

Cook emerged from below, a powder barrel in his arms. I heard something that could've been my name over the wind, and I darted down the stairs as fast as I dared. My limbs shook with exhaustion, but I'd never felt so alive.

"Lad, help me with the cannons," Cook shouted once I'd come close enough to hear. "We'll never get the powder to light in weather like this, and we need to meet them on their terms."

"But I can't—" The thunder and the shouts of the other crewmembers drowned me out. "I can't do spells like that."

Cook laughed and set his barrel down. "Yes, and I don't know any spells stronger than what I need to light my fires. Lucky we've still got these, right?" He held up his hand, where the power-sharing sigils still shone brightly, even now. His smile could've made a feral dog turn around with its tail between its legs. "I figure these were supposed to last until tomorrow. What do you say we put them to good use now?"

My smile grew to match his. Tension coiled in my stomach, but I brushed it off as best I could while Cook loaded the cannons alongside the others. I needed to focus. I'd never bothered learning more than the theory for offensive magic—I had figured I'd never have cause to use it, as most mages hated giving up control of their innate magic to that extent—but it would have to be enough.

I ducked off to the side, in between two cannons, and crouched below the railing. I pictured the most basic fire spell I could, one that turned a spark into an inferno, and silently whispered the words of power. My left hand twitched in the air, moving slowly to draw the runes, while my right hand pressed on the sigil binding Cook's power to me.

The storm raged on, but I hardly noticed it. I retreated into myself, locking out the weather and the chaos alike. I needed to be calm or the spells wouldn't work. The cannons were loaded and the powder primed. Even with my eyes closed, I knew what needed to be done. The runes I still drew in the air thrummed with energy, latching on to the potential stored in the damp powder. When Captain Proulx called for the cannons to fire, I released the spell.

My ears rang as the power thrummed through me. These spells needed less of my attention after they had done their terrible work. The cannons fired once, twice, three times as I repeated the spellwork until my whole body shook. I had no idea if they hit anything, no idea where we stood, but the cannons hadn't stopped firing.

The only thing I knew was that Cook still lived, the wind still screamed, and the battle wasn't over yet.

On we went. My ears had long since deafened to the roar of cannon fire. Even the thunder was as quiet to me as a newborn baby's snore. My face was numb from the biting wind and the pouring rain.

Which was why my eyes shot open when the wind stopped. The Chinese woman knelt in front of me, a bundle of herbs in her hands, and thick bandages around her wrists and forehead. She mouthed something, but I couldn't understand. I shook my head and made to write the runes again, but she grabbed both my wrists in one hand and brought the other to my forehead.

My hearing returned with a crash. I wasn't sure if it was the thunder or the spell, but I'd never heard anything quite so loud. I clapped my hands over my mouth and swore, but she didn't seem to notice.

"Eat this," she yelled over the storm, pulling something from her pocket. "I already gave the conduit his portion."

Before I could even respond, she shoved the bundle into my mouth, and I gagged on the foul taste. I couldn't recognize the specific blend, but the few reagents I did know weren't meant for that. I made to spit them out, and she leaped on me, hand over my mouth.

"Quickly, or they'll catch up!"

I tried to argue, but eventually the need for air and the

urgency of the battle overtook me, and I swallowed them down.

She nodded and jumped up. "You will have more of his strength now. I will tend the others in your place. Get to work!"

I nodded shakily. The herbs churned in my stomach. I didn't know what exactly she'd given me, but I couldn't deny their efficiency. Besides, I doubted she wanted to get caught any more than we did.

Already, Cook's power thrummed under my skin, closer to the surface than even my own abilities. He'd given it to me for the time being, and I needed to use it.

The runes came easier and faster than I'd ever experienced before. Normally I needed to charge them slowly, nursing them with what little ability I possessed, but now it was like a raging river was at my control.

My fingers traced the runes in the air, and they sang a song of destruction. Fire to lick, fire to bite, fire to consume until nothing was left. Other runes followed, ones I hardly remembered, but were deadly in their fervor.

I couldn't let up. If we were caught, I'd either be hanged for piracy or imprisoned forever. My family was relying on me. I couldn't give up yet. My attacks grew more vicious.

Fire followed by lightning followed by ice. The flame consumed the sails, the lightning burned the sailors, and the ice weighed them down. The magic flowed down my hands and raced to the cannons, binding themselves to each speck of powder and each shot. How had Cook never bothered to study? With power like this, any noble would've been falling over themselves to see him trained.

I should've stopped when I tasted blood, but I kept going. As long as the cannons fired, I needed to work. Acid left my hands, ready to eat at whatever it hit first, and it burned my hands as it left.

This was going to destroy me if we didn't stop soon. Cook's innate magic knew I wasn't the one it was meant for, and it would turn against me. The only reason it hadn't happened before now was because he willed it to obey, but that couldn't last forever. There would be a reckoning.

Even now, I could feel it slipping away from me, the river slowing to a trickle. The magic which had shone blindingly a minute ago dimmed. Each rune was weaker than the one that came before it. I fought against the drain, pulling as much toward me as I could.

I wouldn't let the crew down. We'd escape this even if it killed me.

***

Hands caught mine, and my eyes slowly tugged open.

Three blurry figures stood before me. I blinked and squinted, trying to bring them into focus. As the fog gradually cleared, several things occurred to me.

The cannons weren't firing anymore. The rain had changed from a downpour to a drizzle. Captain Proulx, Hakim, and the Chinese woman stood in front of me— although the Chinese woman was the one actually holding my hands in place.

"What happened?" I slurred. My body ached. I doubted I could stand even at gunpoint.

The Chinese woman nodded. "You lived," she said, dropping my wrists and settling into a crouch. "Although I think you'll regret that later."

Captain Proulx knelt at her side and pressed a hand to my forehead. "We escaped. That's all you need to know." She swore and stood. "He's got a fever. Love, can you take him downstairs?"

Hakim nodded. "Alice got Cook downstairs. I can take the boy. Do we have any potions left?"

I opened my mouth to answer, but the Chinese woman

116

beat me to it.

"Thirty healing potions, more anti-nausea potions than anyone would ever need, some iron's breath, and a handful of stamina boosters."

Captain Proulx swore again and rubbed the bridge of her nose. "How long until he's back on his feet? We'll need more than that."

The Chinese woman shrugged. "I don't know. I know alchemy, not flesh. Perhaps your engineers can help?"

I wrestled up the energy to glare halfheartedly at her. Who was she to complain about my potions? I needed all those. Captain Proulx had approved them. I'd have given her a piece of my mind if a roiling in my stomach hadn't threatened to turn foul at that moment.

"Take him to the storeroom," Captain Proulx ordered. "I'll deal with the rest."

Hakim picked me up like a bride on her wedding day without further ado. If I'd been capable of movement, I might have protested, but I had neither the energy nor the desire to waste what little I had on that when I still had questions.

Unfortunately, what little energy I had left wasn't enough to keep me conscious long enough to actually ask any of those questions. The last thing I saw before darkness claimed me was the Chinese woman following Hakim and me below deck.

Chapter 8

I wasn't allowed to leave my cot for three days. This wouldn't have been an issue, except for the numerous people who needed my help.

We'd lost three of the crew in the initial attack. Four more had passed from their injuries in the days since. Less than half the crew had escaped uninjured, and the injured ones that could still walk pulled double shifts alongside them.

We'd gone through my entire backup supply of potions on the first night, while I'd been unconscious. I had reagents, but it would take time to make more when even the tiniest magic use lashed back at me like the most vicious hangover known to any sentient creature that had ever walked the earth.

It was a healer's worst nightmare. Unable to stand at all for the first two days, I directed one of the more educated crewmembers and the Chinese woman through binding injuries and basic poultices. On the third day, I'd been permitted to sit up, and Hakim cleared me to brew potions again, provided I stayed on my cot the whole time.

I worked my fingers to the bone, prepping poultices and preparing reagents that the Chinese woman and Hakim turned into potions. Cook recovered faster than I did—even producing a passable meal the morning after the attack. He was the one to explain where things stood while I ate. The *Seabane* was still in hot pursuit. Our cannons had damaged two of their masts and shredded many of their sails. In turn, the lightning their mage summoned had blown holes in our deck, in our mainsail, and a good portion of the crew. Together, it was enough to keep us just ahead of them, but not entirely out of reach.

We'd been very lucky they hadn't returned our cannon fire. We wouldn't be having this conversation if they had.

The only shred of good news we had was that Kit had made it on board, but even that was tainted. He'd gotten caught in the explosion at the keep and come out of it by the skin of his teeth, albeit separated from the others. Burns covered most of the left side of his body, and he'd broken his arm badly enough that Hakim and Cook had to hold him down while I set it.

"Hakim thinks the magic wasn't stable enough for them to shoot back," Cook informed me as I tore into the salted pork that made up most of today's meal. He settled, rather irreverently, onto the master's chest, which Captain Proulx had ordered put into my storeroom for lack of other places built to hold potentially magical items. In his words, it was the only other place to sit in my storeroom, so that was where his rear end was going. "They must've had a hell of a time convincing their engineers to let the mage on board at all, but I can't imagine they'd allow that and the stress firing the cannons would put on the ship."

I grunted around my food and swallowed bitterly.

The Chinese woman, who'd introduced herself as Li once I woke up and had promptly helped herself to my entire store, snorted. "There are no cannons on that ship," she informed Cook without turning away from her work. "The mage has woven their magic through the sails. It makes the ship heavier, but faster, since they may summon wind and storms to bolster the ship without the use of a trained mage."

I desperately wanted to ask more but didn't dare. For one, I was too weak to move much yet, and it was taking most of my effort to stay in my cot and not try to see what she was doing. For another, I didn't want to upset her. I hadn't seen Fan Ju or Yunru since Li came on board, but something unsettled me about her. I couldn't decide what it was that bothered me, but until then, I didn't want to give her cause to get angry at me.

In the days I'd spent recovering, it had become clear that Li was more than the simple Chinese alchemist she pretended to be. She was far too familiar with the ships and the customs of the Liúwáng to not be part of their clans. And, since the Van der Bergs had trusted her to work on their ships, I wondered why she bothered to hide it at all. By now, everyone knew it, and more than a few private bets had been placed on why and how long she'd hide it.

"How do you know that?" Cook asked, leaning back against the wall. The chest shifted under him but showed no other sign of strain.

Li shrugged and pulled my sack of dragon's wort from its place on the shelf. "Anyone with any magical skill at all knows of that ship. It was a major step forward in shipbuilding. The sails are a work of art."

"It sounds a bit more personal than that." Cook huffed and crossed his arms, trying to look stern, but his smile and the crinkles at the corners of his eyes gave him away.

He'd been in a better mood than I'd seen him since we initially escaped the *Seabane*. With Kit and Alice on board and in relatively good health—at least, once Kit had been persuaded to take one of my stronger healer potions, and what hadn't been healed was suitably bandaged—he had no cause to be upset at the woman who'd thrown all our plans into disarray.

"Van der Berg is quite proud of it. He wished to know more of the design so he could make more ships like it."

"How do you know that?" I asked before I could stop myself. I grabbed some of the remaining pork and took a large bite. "The *Seabane* has been out of this hemisphere for years."

"He told me. It is why he went to such effort to obtain me alongside the ship."

The pork fell out of my hands, and my mouth dropped open. Cook was in no better position. He stared at her like she'd suggested he fill his flask with milk instead of whisky.

"He kidnapped you?" I managed to say. "I knew he was foolish, but I didn't think . . ."

There were reasons for someone to imprison one of the Liúwáng. It was the last option once all other paths had been tried, but it wasn't impossible. Even then, the offender was to be turned over to whatever Liúwáng clan was in the area, and judged by their court. To kidnap one and hold them prisoner unjustly was worse than unthinkable. It was tantamount to suicide. The Van der Bergs were smarter than that, and I'd assumed they'd had an excellent reason for imprisoning Li. Apparently, I was wrong.

"You assumed I was a thief, yes? Perhaps a murderer?" Li let out a bitter laugh and rubbed at the tattoo on her forearm, that of a dragon playing with a rabbit. "The only thing I am guilty of is not trying to leave that hellhole sooner."

Cook pulled out his flask and took a large gulp before he spoke again. "So he had the Keats kidnap you? Feck, we may not need the master's protection. We'll just need to tell the local Liúwáng what he did."

"No," Li shouted. She shot to her feet and turned in practically the same movement, nearly upending the kettle she was using in lieu of a cauldron. "You can't!"

Cook's eyebrows nearly disappeared into his hairline.

"Any reason why, lass?"

She shook her head. "I—I am not Liúwáng. They will not be pleased to hear that Van der Berg thought I was one and asked me about their secrets. They'll punish me."

A laugh broke the silence that followed, and after a moment, I realized it had come from me. "You're joking, right?" I managed to ask once I'd tamed my unexpected giggles. "Do you even know what the Liúwáng will do if they hear we hid something like this from them? Even if you're not Liúwáng"—which I highly doubted— "he still tried to learn Liúwáng secrets. That's enough to bring every Liúwáng-run ship in this hemisphere *and* the Chinese mainland armada down on him. They wouldn't be concerned about you, since you didn't know anything."

Especially considering the other secrets we were currently keeping from them. Between this and Fan Ju's pregnancy, it'd be a miracle if any of us were allowed to fly again.

"We have to tell them. They're the only ones that can stop the Van der Bergs from doing something like this again!"

Li bit her lip and fiddled with the hem of her shirt. "It isn't—" A squeal erupted from the kettle, and she turned to soothe it. She muttered to herself under her breath in rapid-fire Mandarin, and I was exceptionally glad I couldn't understand a word of it.

"It is not the Van der Bergs themselves," she said thickly. "It is one. The eldest son, Johannes."

Shrugging, Cook stood to gather my dishes. "One or all, something like this can't be pushed aside, lass. We need to tell the Liúwáng."

The Liúwáng didn't turn down requests. The current rulers of their homeland were eager to see dissidents, malcontents, and people unfortunate enough to be in the wrong place at the wrong time thrown out, so they didn't have many options. The engineers had even fewer, since they'd traditionally lost their heads to keep the secret of the Liúwáng ships from escaping the borders of China. Zheng Yi Sao had been the one to petition the emperor for permission to organize the criminal engineers, and in turn, her fleet had been a dominating force in the skies for decades. After she retired and returned home, most of the engineers formerly employed by her fleet had nowhere to go. If someone wanted to host a family of Liúwáng in exchange for flying a ship or three? Well, that was just good business sense.

"You said he asked you about Liúwáng ships," I said in a quiet voice once Cook was gone. "You have to know those rules as well as we do."

She shrugged. "I didn't have a choice. I played along at first, requesting trade journals and placing orders for supplies in local newspapers, but eventually he realized what I was doing." She paused and rubbed her wrists. "That was when he began allowing the guards to hurt me."

Snorting, I stretched for a packet of plantain leaf to add to my poultice mix. "Then you have even more cause to tell them." I paused, my tongue catching the next words before they could escape. I couldn't be sure how they hurt her, but in any case, few would want to be that vulnerable in front of strangers. I continued, my voice softer, "We could tell your clan if you don't want to tell the Fortitude Liúwáng about it."

Li stayed silent, and I turned back to my work. With food in my belly, it was easier to focus, and my head hurt less in silence. Still, something about it bothered me.

No one was allowed to know how Liúwáng ships flew. No one was allowed to research Liúwáng methods. And especially, no one was allowed to hurt Liúwáng while trying to learn their secrets. That last bit was enshrined in all Liúwáng contracts to the point that all other commissions, errands, and duties fell aside to preventing information about how their ships worked from reaching other hands.

I knew from personal experience how dedicated they were to keeping their secrets. My father had accidentally stolen a Liúwáng notebook during the affair that got him exiled. He'd returned it, seal unbroken, and they'd still reacted like he'd read the whole thing cover to cover. If he'd never taken that notebook, my life would've been very different.

They could've given him a ten-year ban, perhaps forbidden him from certain parts of Fortitude, and things would've been fine eventually. Instead, he'd been forbidden from flying ever again, his forehead branded, and he'd been threatened with death if he ever got within ten yards of a Liúwáng vessel or engineer. In one drunken evening, he'd destroyed his life and reputation to the point most would rather be killed.

All that to say that if Li said the word, Johannes Van der Berg's death warrant was as good as signed. There wasn't a Liúwáng-run ship in the world that wouldn't do anything they could to see him dead. I wagered his entire family would turn against him, if only to protect their shipping contracts.

She could have her vengeance against whatever indignities he'd forced upon her with ease. All she would have to say was he took her for the express purpose of learning about Liúwáng ships.

But she wanted us to stay silent, even when she knew we couldn't. Whatever she was running from was worse in her mind than what we would face if we kept silent and allowed Johannes Van der Berg to keep whatever information he'd learned.

We worked in silence now. She refused to bend her stance and had shut down when I'd tried to discuss it. The most communication we had was when she handed me ingredients I couldn't reach and I helped her with substitutions for herbs I didn't have. In any other instance, with any other people, it would've been peaceful. Enjoyable even.

It all came crashing down when the door came crashing open, and Fan Ju shoved her way in, a box of vials in her arms.

"Edward, do you have any—" Her scream and the sound of dozens of vials shattering on the ground startled me more than the door flying open.

I jumped up and stumbled to my feet, but Fan Ju shoved right by me. She threw herself at Li and wrapped her in the tightest hug I'd ever seen. Her words exploded in a combination of rapid-fire Mandarin and broken sobs. She pulled back and looked Li up and down, lingering on the bruises and cuts that still littered her face and wrists.

Both seemed to have forgotten I was here, which was exceptionally unfortunate because my legs had already sent me back to the cot.

Li's eyes were the size of saucers. Even if she'd been able to get a word in edgewise while Fan Ju spoke, she didn't seem to be able to speak. She reached out to Fan Ju with a shaking hand and cupped her face. "Mei Mei?" she whispered.

My breath caught in my chest, and it felt like all the air had been sucked from the room.

The feeling got worse when Fan Ju's chatter changed to a single phrase repeated over and over again. "Jiě Jie, Jiě Jie, Jiě Jie . . ."

I knew those words.

But no, it couldn't be. I had to be mistaken. Li was Li. She couldn't be Min Li. We hadn't even had time to look while we were in Leyden. There was no way Alice had just stumbled onto the presumed dead daughter of one of the most important Liúwáng in Fortitude and likely the whole hemisphere.

It couldn't be. It was impossible.

And yet I found myself speaking, and the words came back to me like I spoke them into a long tunnel.

"Fan Ju, is Li your sister?"

Interlude 3

Min Li's recovery changed everything about the mission. Even those who weren't aware of her identity walked with a spring in their steps. Rescuing a Liúwáng engineer would get the entire crew in the good books of the local Liúwáng council. The rewards we'd gain for returning her to her people might not be as visibly valuable as what the master offered us, but it could change the lives of most sailors.

In the brief moments of rest between our work to outrun our pursuers, they openly fantasized about what this would bring them. To be openly declared Liúwáng friends and guaranteed berth on any ship they wanted, higher pay and the patronage of merchants who wanted someone to vouch for them, or even just the fame and the attention it would bring those looking for fair company.

If we survived this, our lives would change for the better, and the crew chose to focus on that instead of the increasing likelihood we'd never see any of that.

The *Seabane* edged closer most days. Their blue sails tainted the far horizon, bringing storms and death with them. We couldn't stop, or their storm would catch us, and yet, hope lingered.

We were getting close to Fortitude. In a perfect world, someone would notice us when we drew near, and they'd alert the master. He'd send his ships and soldiers to fight off the *Seabane*, and we would be victorious heroes, triumphing when all seemed lost.

This was not a perfect world, though, and that cost us dearly.

FORTITUDE'S PRIZE

Chapter 9

Fan Ju refused to let Min Li out of her sight for the next two weeks. At first, it was unbearable. Once I got used to it, though, it was merely intolerable.

Min Li had been sleeping in my storeroom to stay close by in case one of the injured crewmembers needed help while I was incapacitated, and Fan Ju joined her. With all three of us in those cramped quarters, I seriously considered asking Yunru if I could sleep in the bed his wife obviously wasn't using. My storeroom wasn't a large place to begin with, and it felt even smaller now, since Captain Proulx insisted the chest stay there. With all three of us sleeping there, there was barely enough room to breathe. And one of them kept humming, which was driving me crazy.

Complicating matters was that Fan Ju was no longer hiding her pregnancy. At five months along and with a thinner frame, she couldn't have hid it without staying in her quarters the whole time, but she didn't seem to care. With her sister back, her reason for secrecy was gone, and the spells that covered her didn't matter anymore. Still, she refused to trigger any of those spells for reasons she didn't share with me but Min Li agreed with.

The crew took this with varying levels of grace. Most were shocked to the point of needing a drink to calm down, and a handful, the ones with more experience with the Liúwáng, were nearly as alarmed as I had been. Of course, once Cook pointed out that her dying during an attack would almost certainly mean they were dead as well and couldn't be punished, they lightened up.

Min Li herself had been nearly as shocked to discover Fan Ju was pregnant as I had been. Once she got over her surprise at her impending aunthood, many of their conversations took on lecturing tones that made me very glad I only understood a little Mandarin. Even so, it did give me a remarkable amount of glee to see her worriedly counting my anti-nausea potions each day. Vindication was always a wonderful feeling.

When I recovered enough that Hakim and I judged I could move more or less freely again, Min Li's excuses ran dry, but she didn't move into the engineers' quarters. She and Fan Ju still spent all their time in the storeroom, helping prepare potions from my increasingly low supply of reagents and managing the few remaining crewmembers too injured to work but not injured enough to require constant watch.

Cook had taken control of the ones that did require constant watch lest they reinjure themselves trying to work, and had them peeling potatoes in the kitchen while he converted the galley into a massive drying room. The constant drizzle, rainfall, and outright downpours had soaked everything. There were few things more miserable than never being quite dry. The musty odor that had overtaken the ship put much of the crew off their meals altogether.

And, as if we could forget, the *Seabane* still pursued us. I'd nearly forgotten what it felt like to be under the sun thanks to the storms that dogged us day and night. Some days, they nearly caught up, and we fought the weather for each ragged mile. Other days, we could nearly taste freedom.

Today was somewhere in between the two. We could see them on the horizon, but the thunder was a distant rumble instead of a deafening crash.

"We can't stop." Captain Proulx's voice was as ragged and tattered as her ship. She'd pulled the officers and officer equivalents into her cabin to discuss our next move, but we'd been arguing in circles for hours. Even Yunru, who'd convinced Fan Ju and Min Li to take his position so he could attend this meeting, looked ready to throw in the towel and beg his wife and sister-in-law to let him back in.

On the table before us lay the map freshly marked with Fortitude's present location, as determined by tracking spell that morning, and the bare handful of tiny islands between us. A red miniature marked our location, a blue one marked the *Seabane*, and a small rock marked Fortitude itself. The distance between us and our destination was sobering.

"My love, we have no choice," Hakim said gently, reaching over to cover her hand with his. We'd gathered around the table in their stateroom, and they'd claimed the chairs at the far end. Kit, Alice, Yunru, and myself sat elbow to elbow in the few remaining chairs. "There is only so long the crew can patch patches. The bindings on the main mast have held up for now, but we have no idea how long they will stay that way."

Kit nodded listlessly. "Even the dregs have been drained, ma'am. If the main mast falls, they'll catch us anyway. We may as well stop while we still have the ability to get going again." His eyes had been glassy since he showed up, and I glared at him silently. Alice pinned him with a similar glare.

Heaven help me, I was going to drag that man into my storeroom myself if he didn't come willingly. He'd promised me that Cook and Alice were tending to his injuries, but based on her glares, I didn't doubt that Kit had told them a similar story about me. That man was more stubborn about accepting help than any mule I'd ever met.

"I agree," I volunteered, scratching idly at the beard that had the audacity to cover my cheeks after I'd run out of materials to make shaving cream a week into this trek. "We've been lucky so far, but I'm running out of reagents and clean bandages. If anyone else is hurt in these storms, I won't have enough materials to fix them. Most of the islands between us and Fortitude will have some of what I'm looking for." Or at least enough for some basic potionwork.

Captain Proulx rubbed her forehead. Her braids were a frazzled mess, and the bags under her eyes could've held all my reagents effortlessly. The shirt she wore was clearly Hakim's, but she didn't seem to notice beyond rolling the sleeves up. Of all of us, she'd slept the least since our slow race to death began, and it had taken its toll.

"There are only a handful of islands between us and Fortitude," she said firmly. "If we stopped at one of them, the Keats brothers would know. They're not idiots, and even if they were, and we somehow managed to lose them, they'd be between us and Fortitude. They've proven we can't outrun them forever, and we certainly can't beat them in a race when they have a head start."

"We could try power sharing again," I suggested. "I found the recipe for fog-in-a-bottle in the old alchemist's notes. It's a long shot, but I think we could pull it off long enough to confuse them at least. We could repair the main mast once we lost them." We had the right reagents for it, too, if only barely.

"No," Captain Proulx, Hakim, and Kit all said at the same time.

They took a moment to glare at each other. Captain

Proulx won that silent battle, and she spoke again. "Absolutely not. If they catch up to us, we'll be lost in the fog and have a storm to deal with."

"And we can't risk you collapsing again. You nearly burned yourself out last time," Hakim added. He shook his head, frowning. "No, the potential cost would be higher than the payoff. A fog large enough to hide us from the *Seabane* would kill you."

I wanted to protest, but he wasn't wrong. The sigils we'd used for the notice-me-not spell weren't meant for the scale Cook and I had used for the cannons. Innate magic didn't like being manipulated in the same way I manipulated the magic in my reagents and the surroundings to make potions. It would remember me more each time we used the sigils. Besides, Cook might have a solid grasp of letters, but deciphering and then using complicated weather spells was another thing entirely, so it wasn't like he'd be able to produce the spell on his own.

Slumping back in my chair, I mirrored Captain Proulx and rubbed my face. "Then what can we do besides wait for them to catch up?" The exhaustion I'd been pushing back and the lingering weakness from our first fight with the *Seabane* caught up to me all at once, and I desperately wanted to be anywhere else but here.

No one answered. I knew without having to look that they'd all been wondering the same thing.

We were still a week, maybe a bit more, from Fortitude at current speed. We'd pushed the ship to the brink, sailing at speeds we wouldn't have dared normally, and covered the distance in less than half the time it had taken us to get to the Seven Brothers. If the winds held, we'd be able to see Fortitude when the *Seabane* caught up to us, but that was only if the ship didn't fall apart from the stress first.

The dangers we'd faced since we left Fortitude, the losses we'd suffered, none of that would matter.

Whatever the master valued so much in that chest would be lost, again, because we'd failed.

"There is one more option," Yunru said without lifting his eyes from the table. His voice shook, and he'd hidden his hands behind his apron, but it failed to entirely hide how they trembled. "My wife and I would rather not use it, but it seems we're running out of options."

"The spells?" I asked quietly. "But triggering those would mean . . ."

We'd have to hurt Fan Ju and not in a bruises-or-scrapes manner. If we wanted to trigger the spells without the healing magic I couldn't cast, she'd need to be severely injured. A broken limb or something that would make her bleed enough that the strongest potion I could brew wouldn't repair the damage.

And it would put the child at risk. An injury like that might even cause a miscarriage.

"It would bring her mother's people down on us," he said listlessly. "Once she sent word out, every ship within range would be on us like flies on honey." His eyes snapped up to meet Captain Proulx's head-on, and his jaw set. "Even the *Seabane* wouldn't dare attack us then."

If it were any other ship but the *Seabane*, they'd have been safe no matter what. They'd be captured, ransomed, and returned safe and sound. It was just that if the *Seabane* caught us, the engineers would almost certainly be taken back to Johannes Van der Berg, and he had more than enough ships and money to hide Fan Ju if the spells activated while she was under his care. And if Fan Ju and the child survived the experience, they would be leverage over Yunru and Min Li, leverage Johannes Van der Berg would be only too happy to use against them. If they were very fortunate, the master would break his silence and bring proof of his deception and its cost to the Liúwáng, shattering a century's trust and partnership. If they were not, then Fan Ju and Min Li's mother would lose both her children, her son-in-law, and the grandchild she didn't even know was coming.

It had taken the combined armadas of multiple countries to drive the Keats brothers out the first time, when they'd been at their peak. They might only have one ship right now, but they had the backing of one of the most powerful merchants in the world. A man who didn't seem to fear upsetting the order of things.

With the backing of the Liúwáng, we might just manage to escape. But, depending on how their mother took it, this could also cost us the goodwill we'd gain from rescuing Min Li.

And Yunru and Fan Ju would never fly together again no matter what happened.

This was the best option. The only one that wouldn't end with more corpses than survivors.

I knew it. They knew it. Captain Proulx knew it.

She collapsed back in her chair and sighed deeply. "And what does Fan Ju think about this? It's her body on the line."

Yunru sat back in his chair and folded his hands on the table. "She is willing. We have already discussed it. With the assistance of Min Li and Edward, we will be able to tend her and maintain our current course. It will not cost us time or speed." His voice dropped lower and lower with each word until he was practically whispering. "She does not wish for her desires to cost us the ship or worse."

Captain Proulx's eyes squeezed shut, and she took a deep breath, then a second. One hand dropped down to her stomach and pressed against it. The action seemed to calm her. Hakim took her other hand and squeezed it tightly.

Alice and Kit hadn't spoken. From my angle I could see their hands joined together under the table, their matching golden bracelets shimmering in the lamplight.

No matter how this ended, these might be the last few days we all spent together.

"Then we will plan for that," Yunru whispered, his voice steadier than I'd ever heard it in a crowd this size. "I will tell my wife and her sister."

***

I stared moodily into the cloud bank and tugged my hood farther down over my head, quietly humming a half-familiar melody I'd heard someone singing while I was recovering. Thunder rumbled in the distance, and I cast an eye to glare at the *Seabane* on the horizon as a fresh drizzle replaced the light mist that had dampened us most of the afternoon.

If I never saw a storm again and the entirety of the islands went into drought, I thought I would've died a happy man. Perhaps I should find a berth on a ship bound for the African Sky after this. I'd heard it rarely rained there.

A part of me wanted to go back inside, but I would lose my mind if I stared at the four walls of my storeroom any longer, no matter how much my limbs ached and begged for sleep. Over the past few weeks, I'd had my fill of that. I needed to be anywhere else for the time being.

Min Li and I had officially used the last of my healing reagents. With them, we brewed the most powerful potion we could, preparing for the inevitable. It might not cure Fan Ju entirely, but she would be stable when their mother found us and hopefully still pregnant. That was the important part if any of us wanted to keep sailing.

Min Li disappeared with the potion after we finished it, leaving me to wrestle Kit into submission. He'd disappeared before I could get my hands on him after the meeting, but Cook and Alice dragged him in once Min Li left. He'd grumbled the whole time that he was fine and all this was unnecessary.

Fine, by his definition, meant the beginning of a raging infection. I gave him credit where it was due; he'd bound the injuries well enough, but without personal attention, he hadn't realized some of the burns had started to fester in the constant damp.

I'd forced the weakest of the healing potions I had left down his throat followed by about half of Cook's flask, and then had Cook and Alice hold him down while I cleaned and sanitized his burns. Cook said Kit would forgive me one day, but for now, it was good that I was able to teach them how to handle Kit's ongoing care. Alice just said he disliked the taste of potions and that he hated to be a bother. The man himself had grumbled at both of them and glared at me.

I resisted hitting him for that, if only because I didn't want to undo all my hard work. If I, a member of a guild known to produce poor patients in the best of times, was able to submit myself to another's treatment, he had no excuse.

And Min Li had done a phenomenal job while I'd been unconscious. She was a skilled alchemist—even more so than Fan Ju—because she was familiar with Western and Chinese alchemy. It had been fascinating to watch her work as I recovered. The way she made herself at home among my books and equipment had bothered me after I initially woke up, but I was grateful for it now. I'd learned a lot. Not many could have kept so many people alive with damp reagents, bandages, and people. Even that blasted songs she kept humming didn't bother me anymore.

We'd spoken a lot when I'd been trapped in my cot. Nothing serious, mostly about the health of patients I couldn't see and how I wanted them treated, but also about the differences in our preferred styles of alchemy. It had been comfortable, enjoyable even. I hadn't met many alchemists my age, and it was thrilling to be able to discuss the craft with someone who understood it even better than I did.

"The deck will still be wet if you catch the rain, Edward." Min Li's rough voice startled me from my thoughts, and I jerked away. She let out a huff of laughter and took my place at the railing. "May I ask why you're out in this weather?"

I shrugged and moved to the side. I had no particular attachment to that part of the deck. "It's nothing," I said in a low voice. "I just needed some air." My attempts to lean casually on the railing next to her failed miserably because my elbow betrayed me. It slipped on the damp wood, and then my feet failed to find purchase in the puddles. I stared up at the sky and at Min Li's quietly laughing eyes and wished briefly that I'd never been born.

Blushing furiously, I was grateful for my hood as she pulled me back to my feet. "Thanks," I muttered once I had stable footing again.

"It is no trouble," she said demurely. "And I am grateful for the opportunity to laugh."

"Happy to help." I desperately willed my blush to die down, but my cheeks stubbornly stayed flamed. At least something good had come of my embarrassment. "Anyway, why are you out here? Where's Fan Ju? Aren't you two attached at the hip these days?"

Min Li ducked her head and looked away. "I also needed air," she said shortly. "My sister agreed that I should seek it, and you were not in your storeroom."

Ah.

"You don't like the plan, do you?" I asked quietly, drawing closer and lowering my voice even though all crew with sense had long since moved below deck to escape the rain. Even the pixies had crept back into their nests.

I'd grown more comfortable with Min Li than was perhaps wise, considering my family history, but I couldn't help it. Min Li was smart and clever, and I liked knowing that she sought me out when she was having issues with her sister.

She snorted. "Would you if one of your siblings were the bait?" She lowered her head and dug a nail into the railing. "She insists this is the only way and refuses to listen to reason."

My chest hurt, and I swallowed against the lump that grew. There was little I wouldn't do to protect my siblings. It was why I was here, after all. "Isn't that what younger siblings do best?" I asked hoarsely. Bloody hell, no, this wasn't the time for homesickness. "My mother always said it was their job to drive the oldest wild."

Min Li's nail carved a line into the paint, and she grunted. "She has always done that. Our mother coddled her. She still thinks this will be solved like a fairy story." Her voice broke, and she swallowed back tears. "She thinks our mother will solve everything, like she did when we were children. She thinks she and the child will escape this with little harm and not . . ." Her breath hitched, and she took three heaving breaths.

It wasn't my place to push her to keep going, so I didn't. She continued anyway.

"Mother always listened to her. I was expected to be the good daughter, the one who would marry well, have strong children, and take over when Mother was ready to step down. Fan Ju ran wild, and I was expected to bite my tongue and now—"

I pretended not to hear her quiet gasping breaths.

"Is that why you left?" I asked in a low voice, not really expecting an answer.

I understood what she meant to a degree. I was the oldest in my family with all that it entailed. When my father started his downward spiral, I'd had to pick up the slack. Between my apprenticeship and the farm, my childhood ended much earlier than my siblings'. I'd always been expected to give more than they had been.

It had stung then, to watch them play during festivals and celebrations while I helped Mother package hangover cures and prepare fireworks, but I would admit that my pockets were always fuller than theirs when the merchants came to visit. Mother had tried to soothe my aches even if she couldn't stop their cause. If it hadn't been for that . . . by the isles, I'd probably have found berth on the first ship away from St. Bernard's after I finished my apprenticeship.

"I didn't . . . I wasn't planning to stay away forever," she said quietly. "I just needed a break. After Fan Ju's wedding, I felt I would scream if I had to entertain one more of the suitors Mother picked, and I begged to begin my journeymanship early. I wanted a break from being the heir, from being her daughter. I just wanted to be me for a while."

I'd heard part of this story before. Fan Ju told me that her sister had joined a ship a few months after her wedding. Min Li and their mother had fought about it for ages before their mother had finally allowed it. The ship had been attacked a few months after it left Fortitude, and well, I knew how that ended.

"It's okay," I said softly, turning up to look at the sky.

"You don't have to tell me."

But maybe she did. Maybe all the stress that she'd been fighting with since before she left wanted an outlet before we died, and she'd take whatever she found. She shook her head, and her hood fell off her shoulders. The rain had turned back into a drizzle that slowly soaked her hair.

"Van der Berg was behind it. He hired the pirates that attacked us, and had another vessel waiting to take me after I fell off the ship." Her voice broke. "I was relieved for a while. I worked on his ships, improving them as much as I could. I didn't have to be an heir or my mother's daughter while I was there. He didn't know who I was, he just wanted someone to study the *Seabane* and—"

She stopped with a gasp. Her grip on the railing turned her knuckles white, and her breaths came quick and short. "He wouldn't let me leave. When I finished with the ship and wanted to bring my knowledge to the local clans, I tried to go, but he wouldn't let me. He wanted to keep me and my knowledge for himself."

I recognized this. I hadn't studied mind healing like my mother had, but I'd seen this before. People who'd undergone trauma sometimes got stuck there by their minds, like someone who couldn't stop pressing a bruise to reassure themselves it was still there.

"Min Li, if this is bothering you, you should stop." That wasn't the right thing, this wasn't how to help. I had known what to do once, but the treatment eluded me. Shaking her wouldn't help, and I didn't want to bring her breakdown to the others' attention. We needed to ground her. My hand found hers, and I squeezed it tightly. *You're here*, I silently tried to communicate, *you're here and not back there.*

"He said he needed better ships and that the master knew Liúwáng secrets, but he couldn't open that stupid chest, and he thought I could and—" She took a ragged breath, and her hand clenched around mine. She continued like that, gasping for breath and holding on to my hand like it was the only thing keeping her on the ship, for what felt like ages, and I could do nothing more than provide silent support.

"Look," she managed to say, each word choked with tears. A broken laugh escaped her and was swallowed by another sob. "The rain stopped."

That . . . hadn't been what I was expecting, but now that I paid attention, she was right. The clouds were breaking apart, even as I watched. Min Li's death grip on my hand turned into her head resting on my shoulder as she silently wept.

My mind whirled as I wrapped her in my arms, my desire to comfort someone I hoped could be a friend overwhelming my supreme discomfort with the situation.

This wasn't right. We hadn't been free of the rain for weeks. Just a few hours ago, we'd been arguing about how the *Seabane* would catch us, but I couldn't even see it on the horizon. I whispered mindless comforts and kept looking, searching desperately for something I knew should've been there but wasn't.

I wasn't eased by the crew on watch calling out the news, and Min Li pulled away, dabbing at her tears with her cloak. The others hidden below deck emerged to a glorious sunset, and their cheer was palpable, but I couldn't shake a deep feeling of unease, one I knew the others would share when they stopped to think about it.

There was no way we could outrun the *Seabane*, and they never gave up, which begged the question:

Where had they gone?

Chapter 10

We sailed under clear skies for three days with no sight of the *Seabane*. With no storms to contend with, we were able to complete the hull and deck repairs while on the move, and our time had much improved. We even managed a few hours' stop to brace the mast. Admittedly, Cook had needed to sacrifice most of the benches and tables in the galley to do so, but we were almost whole again. By my measure, between the tail wind and the repairs, we'd cut our travel time in half. We should be within sight of the shipping lanes in a few hours, and Fortitude wouldn't be far away after that.

It was unnerving. We'd spent the last three weeks on the edge of a storm, waiting for the other shoe to drop and the *Seabane* to swoop in. Somehow, this was worse.

According to all the stories I'd ever heard, the *Seabane* never gave up a target, and we were still far enough from Fortitude that no one would've seen them attack. They had to have done the same calculations we had done. It made no sense for them to retreat. We all knew it, even if none of us verbalized it. Something had happened, and if we couldn't figure out what, we'd be caught with our pants down.

The tension had the crew walking on a knife-edge.

The only ones who didn't seem to mind were the engineers. With the *Seabane* gone and the miles between us and Fortitude slowly disappearing, they had no need to trigger the tracking spells on Fan Ju. She and her child were safe as long as the *Seabane* didn't reappear.

Or at least, that was my assumption. Min Li hadn't spoken with me since the *Seabane* disappeared, even though I'd seen her around the ship, chatting with Fan Ju or Yunru. I tried not to mind. She'd been through something awful and was likely mortified about breaking down in front of a stranger. It was for the best that we went our separate ways anyway.

At least, that's what I told myself whenever that small part of me mourned our conversations.

The hours inched by, crawling like the weight of our sorrows and expectations had nailed the hands of time in place. Mine weren't the only eyes glued to the horizon, searching for some sign our odyssey was at an end or our enemies had reappeared. Tasks were done by rote, and everyone who could looked for reasons to linger on deck.

The inevitable happened with Fortitude in sight, just as the tension that wound tight around all our hearts loosened its suffocating grip.

"Sails! Hostile sails on the horizon!" The lookout's screams split the air as soundly as a lightning strike would rend the earth.

Sprinting up to the top deck, fighting against the others, I desperately prayed that the lookout was mistaken. That an oddly shaped cloud or merchant's ship had somehow been mistaken for our worst nightmare.

It wasn't to be. When I reached the back railing, scanning the horizon, my heart dropped from my chest and took all my strength with it. There, less than ten miles away and emerging from a darkening cloud bank, was the familiar rounded sails of the *Seabane*. Behind it . . .

A whole fleet, perhaps as many as fifteen ships, each bearing dark blue sails crackling with contained lightning. They cut the clouds apart like the weather had no hold on them, eating up the short distance between us like hell was licking at their heels and a hurricane followed behind them. I looked at them and wanted to weep.

Those were mage ships, and there were still twenty miles between us and Fortitude. Unless the captain had a miracle hidden away somewhere, we had no chance of surviving. There was no way we could beat them there.

Stumbling back from the railing, I turned to the helm, where Captain Proulx and Hakim had made their stand. Captain Proulx's head hung low, something like fear darkening her face, while Hakim was resigned. They knew the odds as well as any other sailor.

Captain Proulx noticed for the first time the others staring at her, awaiting orders they knew wouldn't save them. She glanced at Hakim, who squeezed her hand, and the fear disappeared.

Resolution took its place.

"We're not done yet," she snarled, throwing her coat and hat aside. "All hands to stations. Someone tell the engineers we need as much speed as they can give us. Hakim—"

Hakim took over from his wife without a second thought. "Toss anything we don't need. The hammocks, the ballast, the extra food."

Invigorated—or perhaps simply eager for someone else to take their survival in hand—the crew leaped into action. Half formed a line and handed crates, barrels, and anything else we could find up to the deck and over the side into the sea far below us. The others took to the rigging, working each scrap of momentum we could from the wind and freeing the griffins so they at least would survive this. Anyone not occupied with speed took to the cannons, priming them for battle.

I found myself in the line, throwing every ounce of strength I had into our work.

Lighter. We needed to be lighter. With the storm and time against us, we needed to dump every pound we could, and I wasn't about to let us fail because of my fear. Crates and books and cloth, even Cook's pots and pans, all went over the edge. The ship shuddered and groaned, but slowly and surely picked up speed.

We were within sight of Fortitude. At this speed, we'd hit the docks too fast to stop, but we were nearly there. The guards would see us, and we could claim sanctuary. But despite our increased speed, the mage ships and the *Seabane* were faster. It felt like I could reach out to touch them.

In the few moments I could spare, I'd kept an eye on them. The unlanded flag that had alarmed me those few short weeks ago was nowhere to be seen. The Keats brothers had made their loyalty known, and their master wasn't one to be thwarted. Johannes Van der Berg had thrown his entire force behind reclaiming his ill-gotten goods, and he didn't care to hide it.

I willed the ship faster, willed Fortitude closer, and prayed that whatever spellwork or alchemy powering the unholy speed devouring the distance between us would fail catastrophically. We were almost there. If we could just get within the water, within the master's territory, we'd be safe.

I knew the moment our pursuers got into range. The air itself shook with rage when dozens of cannons fired all at once, fire and ice and acid coating each ball. The spells propelling them gave them speed and vigor, but not accuracy. At this distance, most missed. The few that hit crashed through the hull below, and many hands that had been lightening the ship turned to saving what was left.

We made it through two more volleys before they really hit us. Captain Proulx and Hakim had commandeered one of the surviving cannons while Cook and Kit took the remaining two. I made myself useful by doing what I did best. I tore shirts for bandages and patched unfortunate survivors in between hauling ammunition and powder to the cannons. The booms and echoes of the cannon volleys deafened me to anything but the screams of my patients. My world narrowed to what was in front of me. I couldn't worry about our pursuers or Fortitude when there were people who needed my help right now.

I was bandaging a burn when the world turned on end. I came to lying flat out on the deck, my ears ringing like a bell had gone off in my skull and my vision spinning like a top. My mind wandered and swam, darting back and forth, trying to work out if I was still whole or not and what I needed to do in either case. The deck around me burned and acrid smoke filled my lungs.

Someone was screaming. I didn't think it was me, but my mind refused to focus on anything more than that. It was my job to stop the screaming. Someone needed my help, and here I was, lying on the ground like a lummox.

We'd been hit. I stared sightlessly into the dark clouds above us, mind spinning in useless circles while it tried to catalog more than that. The heavens let loose their burdens, and the rain hit us like a club. It was enough to jolt me back into something resembling motion.

Breathing deeply through my mouth, I shook my head and counted to three. The world came back into focus, and I let out a hollow cry.

The helmsman lay next to me, which was very wrong. He was supposed to be on the upper deck, but he was down here, next to me, and a piece of railing pinned him to the deck. Blood pooled beneath him, and he let out a last gurgling breath as I watched. It should've unnerved me, but it didn't. He was dead and I couldn't fix that.

I stumbled to my feet and frantically spun around. I wasn't sure where I was going, but I was needed. Others lay dead and dying around me, but the ship was still moving. The cannons, which had miraculously escaped the onslaught, roared as Captain Proulx and Hakim ran between them. Alice was nowhere to be seen, the griffins had long since vanished, and Kit was frantically digging through a pile of what used to be the portside stairs, his mouth moving in a scream I couldn't hear.

The edge of the water taunted me just past Kit's shoulders. Boats and people moved like ants, scurrying over the docks and onto the ships. They'd seen us. They knew we were coming. It remained to be seen what reception we would receive by bringing a fleet to their doorsteps, but they knew we were here.

My face split into a feral grin, and I let out a victorious shout. We were almost there. If we could just make the water—

My joy turned to terror as the ship slowly turned right. I spun around, terror seizing my limbs, and froze. The helmsman, still pinned to the ground, lay beside me. The wheel, our only chance of escaping this, spun wildly. Captain Proulx hadn't noticed yet, or if she did, couldn't tear her attention from the defenses long enough to correct it.

I took a step forward before I really thought about it, stumbling through blood and over corpses that had been friends when I woke up this morning. I didn't look down.

Someone needed to guide the wheel. Everyone on deck was either occupied, dead, or dying. What crew had sense left had fled below deck, away from the chaos, to deprive the Van der Berg fleet of any more targets. They'd be close enough for guns soon. I could practically smell them from here.

The starboard stairs were still intact. Whatever blow that had taken the helmsman had spared them, and I stumbled toward them like a drunkard seeking salvation in the bottom of his next bottle. Through rain and blood and debris, I climbed up. The ringing in my ears overtook everything else. The world quieted and stilled, narrowing to me and the wheel.

I caught its jagged spokes midspin, and my arm burned from the strain of redirecting it. The blow that killed the helmsman had ripped half of the wheel away, but it still moved. I spun it windward, back to Fortitude, and prayed.

We were too close to stop now. The edge of the water disappeared behind us, and the docks loomed in front of us. If we hit the water, we'd hit the dock at full speed. If we didn't, we'd hit the town instead.

While I stood, frozen in fear and indecision, Fortitude took my choice from me. Two dozen ships and fishing boats of all sizes took flight nearly as one and charged forward, making up in numbers what they lacked in firepower. The docks moved, people packed so tightly upon them that they might as well have become a living carpet. My panicked mind wondered briefly if the ships of Fortitude intended to shoot us down before we hit the dock, but they flew past us and right into battle.

The world returned with a pop, and ragged cheers and clanging bells replaced the echoing silence I'd lived in before now. The few crew left on deck had collapsed, sobbing and shouting, and if it weren't for my position, I'd have joined them.

Kit dug Cook from the rubble and dragged his bleeding body across the deck. Captain Proulx hugged Hakim, who clutched his arm that had to be broken to his chest and— the docks loomed in front me as thousands of victorious cheers turned to terror.

I pulled with all my might, bringing the ship up as high as I could and to the starboard side. It groaned in my hands, fighting our inertia and its own weakening structure.

This wasn't over yet. I couldn't turn around, and we were too close to land. A shot whistled past my head, crashing into the lower deck, and I swore violently at the wheel. The docks still thrived, even with a hundred people now in the water, so the ground was not a landing option, and the water had become a battlefield. We couldn't stop, and we couldn't go anywhere but up, so that's where I went.

We dropped speed dramatically as we climbed, but it wasn't enough for my taste. With each turn and twist, we skimmed the rooftops of the buildings below us. Unfortunately, even if we did stop, there wasn't anywhere we could go. The streets were too narrow, the buildings too flimsy, and the markets crowded with dedicated merchants and customers that wouldn't let anything like an invasion keep them from their commerce.

"The keep! Edward, make for the keep!" Hakim's voice broke through the thunder and the crash of battle. I looked down at him, and he waved me on, pointing toward the dark building that loomed over the whole island.

"Why?" I yelled back. I jerked the wheel to the right once more, swearing at whatever moron had decided their clock tower needed to go right where we were headed. The keep would have some open space for sure, but they had a massive wall around them too. The only place we'd be able to land would be the massive walkway in front.

"The gate's big enough for a dragon," he answered, ramming the rod down a cannon with one hand. "It has to be. We're smaller than that."

"But we're still going too fast!"

"Just do it," Captain Proulx yelled, wiping a hand through the ash and powder coating her dark skin. "That's an order."

I don't understand, I wanted to scream back. We'd managed to make it this far with most of our skins intact. Between the wind, the rain, and our present speed, going for the keep would be a death wish. Even though the gate was wider than us, we'd barely fit through even if we scraped the ground. It'd be like trying to thread a needle with a rigging rope while jumping off a building.

"Bardsley!"

The deck shook, and I knew without having to look that we'd been hit again. I chanced a look behind us and nearly let go of the wheel in fright. One of the Van der Berg ships was right behind us, so close I could see the smoke coming off their cannons.

I hesitated, then swore as violently and colorfully as I knew. We were dead either way.

The ship fought me. Speed was not on our side, and the sudden direction changes were straining the damaged hull. But still, up we climbed, toward the keep. I could see the gate Hakim mentioned, already wide open and lit up like a harvest festival. They couldn't have made a better mark if they'd circled it with red paint. If we managed to stop before we hit the wall opposite the gate, we might actually get through this.

There was another problem though. In my efforts to escape the ship chasing us, I'd climbed too high. Dropping at this speed might get us down, but like a bird of prey, we'd also speed up. If I turned around, tried to approach from a different angle, perhaps the heavens would be merciful and we'd get another chance, but I doubted we would have that much time, and each moment we were out like this left us sitting ducks.

My hand caught once more on a broken spoke, and a surge of energy thrummed through me.

My breath caught, and I grinned a terrible grin. I knew what had caused that energy, and through it, I might just be able to solve both issues in one go.

It took a greater alchemist than me to make a ship fly. The runes were complex and confusing, and to be given life—to keep the ship up when nature demanded it return to earth—took magic like none I would ever know. It was a great machine with hundreds of moving parts. Even then, they needed something more before the Liúwáng magic or a mage's power could truly bring the ship aloft.

I would never be able to power or break those runes on my own. But to disrupt them, alter them for just a moment? That was an alchemist's bread and butter. Even I could do that.

My fingers found the runes carved along the inside of the wheel, and I pushed forward with all my power, suggesting, for a moment, that the runes here reach out to their kin. That they stop exerting their will on wood and metal and rope and that nature be allowed to take its course again.

Gravity took effect immediately. The ship dropped like a stone for three terrifying seconds before the runes brushed my influence aside and fought to rise, struggling to regain the position I'd forced them to abandon. I swallowed back bile and tasted blood and rain on my lips. When had my nose started to bleed? No matter, that wasn't the issue at hand. I spared a moment of pity for those below deck, who would have no idea what was going on. Gritting my teeth, I touched the rune again, and we dropped.

The shots of our pursuer went wide each time we dropped. By the time they readjusted their aim and could fire again, it was too late. I let out a throaty wild laugh. They'd be too close to fire again without risking damage to themselves soon.

The ship shuddered and groaned each time I persuaded the runes to stop, but it was working. Captain Proulx caught my wild eyes, and I jerked my head toward the gate. We were so close. I had it under control.

Trust me, I silently begged. It wasn't like there were a lot of options at this point.

Her eyes could've been dinner plates, but she nodded. The bodies and injured had been cleared from the deck, and it was just the three of us. She kept my gaze, and deep sorrow filled her face. She took Hakim's hand as I pressed my fingers to the rune once more, and then they bolted toward the upper deck, toward me when we stopped falling.

I wanted to scream at them, to beg them to flee for the safety of below deck, but a sharp pain shot through my brain in time with the thrumming of the runes. They should go down, not up here with me, where a rogue shot or a sudden stop couldn't throw them across half the city.

They reached me before I could make us fall again. Hakim took the wheel from me while Captain Proulx fastened ropes around our waists.

"Keep doing whatever you were doing," she grunted, tying the ropes tightly to the mast behind us. "It's confusing them."

"I need the runes," I rasped out, my hands belatedly joining her in testing the knots. This was smart. I should've had a lifeline the whole time. "I can't reach them otherwise."

Hakim grunted and forced the wheel left. He had more grace about it than I did, even with a broken arm. Likely because he actually knew how to steer a ship the size of the *Vulturnus*. "We only need a few more drops. Come around to the other side of the wheel, you should be able to reach the runes there."

His head spun around, and he pinned Captain Proulx with a wild look. "Can you keep a watch? We took too many hits while we were getting up here."

She darted forward and planted a kiss on his cheek. Her grin was something inhuman. "Of course. It'll be like that season we spent in Barbados."

Hakim's face softened, and he turned back to the front. "Get ready. Wait for the captain's call."

He didn't need to tell me again. With the adrenaline ramping up, my whole body buzzed with energy. I slid in front of the wheel, leery of the broken railing and the blood that coated the area there, and pressed my hand firmly against the largest of the revealed runes.

Captain Proulx called to Hakim twice, and he listened without questioning her, swerving to avoid fire from our pursuer or missed volleys from the battle in and around the harbor. Unquestionably, they were much better at this than I was. Even without dropping the magic keeping us going, Hakim had slowed us down and dropped us more evenly than I'd managed to do even once. It was fascinating to watch, in a way that only the likely concussed soul could appreciate.

The screams of frustration behind us were audible, even over the slowly increasing distance between us. More than half the shots that had previously littered the deck or scattered past me missed entirely. By now, they must know what we intended. If they didn't get us in their next volley, they wouldn't have another chance. Their ship was a lot bigger than ours, after all.

The gate came up between one heartbeat and the next. One moment, Hakim and Captain Proulx were directing

154

us back and forth, between the roofs that were closer now than I'd ever been, and the next, the gate loomed in front of us.

"Drop!" Captain Proulx's scream reverberated around the shattered deck, and I moved on instinct, the magic flowing through the tiny channels within me and breaking the edges of the runes.

We fell, passing through the gate and the tunnel that followed. The tallest mast splintered and broke against the ceiling, littering the deck and the ground behind us. As we emerged from the darkness and into the light on the other side, I collapsed, my whole body shaking. I let out a victorious crow and howled at the sun.

We'd made it. We'd threaded the needle and beat the clock.

The ship slowed to a stop, hovering in the air like a giant wooden bee. Even with my hands free of the runes, I felt the magic slipping away, and a deep, keening loss ripped through me.

The *Vulturnus*, having ferried its crew home one last time, was simply too damaged to keep going. The splint we'd used to reinforce the mast lost the battle against gravity, and the mast had fallen into the one behind it, which in turn snapped off sails and ropes alike when it succumbed to the damage dealt by our pursuers. I didn't even want to think about what had been done to the hull, which was by far the largest target.

"Edward!" Hakim's horrified yell broke me from my celebration and my mourning, and I jerked up. The ship shuddered one last time and dropped the last few feet, slamming into the ground with all the grace of a whale fall and listing to the left side.

My whole body ached and protested each move like I was trying to swim through stone. I slid left, and my scrambling fingers refused to latch onto anything. My flesh fought against me like it had used the last of my energy in getting us here, and now it refused to put forth any more effort than necessary to keep me alive.

A sharp tug around my waist was the only thing that stopped me from falling off and over the edge. The lifeline, merciful heaven, I'd completely forgotten about that.

"Bardsley, are you all right?"

I followed the sound of Captain Proulx's voice and saw her and Hakim clinging to opposite sides of the now-broken mast.

My throat ached and refused to work just yet, so I settled for nodding.

"Good, don't move, I'll come to you." Using her lifeline as a harness, Captain Proulx slowly walked down the crooked deck toward me. It clung oddly under her stomach. "Love, see if anyone below deck needs help."

Dully, I wondered if we shouldn't be more concerned about the battle outside. They'd all come here chasing us, after all.

Perhaps Captain Proulx thought the master would keep us safe, I mused as she untied my lifeline. She slid me to the railing, and I crumpled into a heap against what was left of it. It groaned alarmingly under my weight.

It turned out Hakim didn't need to check on the crew, because they spilled out from their hiding places before he managed to work his way to the deck. The relatively whole helped the more injured crawl up the off-kilter stairs and from there to the ground. Distantly, I noted that the majority would need medical care. I doubted any of my potions or equipment had survived intact, so I'd need to find more elsewhere. Perhaps Mcl would have some they'd be willing to part with for a good price, or at least lend me until I received my pay for this endeavor.

My limbs still weren't responding right though—or at all, really—so perhaps Mel would have to attend to me first. Even in my addled state, I knew enough to know I should be concerned about that. That being said, in the grand scheme of things, the way the world spun with each movement was much more interesting.

Captain Proulx slid down next to me. "Can you stand?"

"I doubt it," I croaked, having finally worked up enough saliva to wet my throat. "The world won't stop moving."

She hummed and frowned at my akimbo limbs. Her eyes traveled back up my face, and her frown got even deeper. "I don't doubt that."

Now in a vaguely upright position, I had a much clearer view of what was left of the ship and the crew.

The ones that could still stand were armed with a mix of firearms and sharp implements. One, I noted, had grabbed Cook's cleaver and held it in front of them like a shield. If I'd had the energy or the voice, I'd ask them if they were more concerned about whatever attacker got through gates than they were with Cook if he found out his cleaver had been used for something besides cooking.

Yunru and Min Li emerged with Fan Ju held between them. They, at least, looked relatively unharmed. It made sense, since the engineers' quarters were almost always the best-defended on the ship.

I say relatively, because Fan Ju had clearly taken the worst of things. Her face was whiter than chalk, and her right arm was wrapped in bloodstained silk—perhaps how the Fortitude ships had known to come when they did— while her left leg was braced with wood and cloth. The leg was likely broken, in my professional—albeit confused— opinion, and badly, too, if she'd taken the potion that Min

Li and I made and the potion hadn't healed it and the cut all the way. Assuming the potion had survived the chaos long enough to be drunk, at least.

Hakim and Kit organized the crew too injured to walk in neat rows close to the ship. Those that could still walk were directed through basic first aid by Kit and myself, once Kit propped me up on a barrel so I could supervise and he'd bandaged the worst of my injuries.

Apparently, I'd hit my head when the deck exploded, which was why the world felt off-kilter. It also explained where all the blood on my shirt had come from and why my nose kept bleeding if I turned my head too far in any direction. My ribs hurt quite a bit as well, and the world kept going worryingly gray at the edges, but I figured we could put off looking at those until we'd stopped everyone else from bleeding to death.

Min Li did not let my injuries persuade her to take it easy on me. Her rant about "disrupting engine integrity" and "putting all of us at risk" would've been enough to drive me out of alchemy altogether if I remembered any more of it than that.

I still wasn't sure what was happening beyond the walls of the keep, but if the distant booms and crashes were any indication, fighting was still happening. From my angle, I could see that a thick metal portcullis had fallen over the gate, blocking us from going back that way, even if the ship hadn't been a very large lawn decoration at the moment.

No one came out to greet us, which I thought was odd in the moments my mind broke free from the mist covering it. There was no way the entire keep's staff had joined the defense of their city and that any who'd stayed behind hadn't noticed an entire ship crashing through their front door.

The sounds of fighting died away eventually, presumably either over or too far away to hear from here, although I couldn't say when, since the minutes and hours blurred together. I hoped for the first, because the storm clouds had cleared, and I was enjoying the sun on my skin.

My answer came soon enough.

The portcullis lifted, and a dark shape emerged from the other side. It came into the light, and many of the crew let out terrified shouts.

I wasn't among them, but only because I recognized what it was and I knew my local history.

That was a dragon. A male dragon, if the patterns on his tattered wings were any indication. He pulled himself through the gate, and we were treated to his full glory. The glitter of sunlight on his ebony scales, the thick scarring around what was left of a hind leg, and the entire mast in his mouth.

I smiled dopily up at him, and my head lulled to the side. "Hello, sir," I shouted as loud as I could. "Nice of you to let us dock here."

The master's lips pulled back in a horrifying grin. He dropped the mast, which crashed to the ground, nearly hitting the *Vulturnus* in the process. "Well, I do appreciate it when my parcels are delivered to me directly."

Chapter 11

The master was more than generous to his employees, no matter how close they were to the end of their contract. Or at least, that's what Hakim told me when he came to see me after the healer, Madame Chén, cleared me for visitors more than three weeks after we crashed through the keep's front gate.

The master paid for our lodging in the city, healers for our injured, and insisted on financing the reconstruction of the *Vulturnus*. His generosity even influenced the local merchants, all of whom forgave us for bringing a fleet upon their town when they saw how he and the Liúwáng favored us. The townsfolk were occasionally less generous, but Hakim told me that they held their tongue for the most part. One did not protest when the Liúwáng demanded action, after all.

Captain Proulx was now drowning in merchants eager to have the captain of the ship that stormed the keep and raided the Van der Bergs working for them. Having been raised a merchant herself, she'd spent every moment since we'd returned wooing them and getting concrete contracts in exchange for a few vague promises on her part. If Hakim told the truth, the next three years' worth of commissions were already set in stone and at very favorable rates.

"So do we know when the ship will be ready to sail again?" I asked, picking at my scone. The master favored healers in the noble district, and I was very glad the payment wasn't coming from my pocket. I'd be bankrupt

160

if I tried. I'd seen this tea set in a shop window once, and the price tag was more than what my mother's shop made in three months. I didn't even want to think about the price of the potions, reagents, and spells Madame Chén used on me.

Hakim shrugged and delicately sipped from his cup. He'd come to visit me a few times, and I looked forward to each visit for the knowledge he brought and for his company. Madame Chén, a venerable Chinese woman who'd been practicing alchemy longer than my mother had been alive, was fantastic at her work but was too busy to spend long periods chattering with a lonely alchemist. Hakim was often the only person I spoke with all day.

"At least six months." He shook his head and laughed, either from amusement or frustration, I couldn't really tell. "The master insists he will spare no expense to get the *Vulturnus* back to top shape, but even with his not inconsiderable magical ability and the support of the Liúwáng, a ship is not built in a day."

And who knew how long the winds would blow favorably for us. He didn't say that, but it was clear he was thinking it. At this point, it'd be better if the master just gave us a ship from his fleet. We'd be back in the sky sooner.

"And the rest of the crew?" I'd only seen a handful since Madame Chén cleared me for visitors. Alice stopped by with apologies for Cook and Kit, who were confined to their quarters in no uncertain terms until they were fully healed, and there'd been a few of the others that worked on my shift, but that was it. I hadn't even seen Fan Ju or Min Li since we returned.

I'd seen their family's doctor, of course. He'd ambushed me once I was coherent again, and he grilled me about everything I'd given her during her pregnancy and everything I could remember of her symptoms. My logbook, unfortunately, had been one of the items tossed during the chase, or I was fairly certain he'd have just demanded all the pages pertaining to Fan Ju and Min Li. He didn't seem to like talking to me. In fact, I was fairly certain that he'd have killed me himself if I were the only one who knew about Fan Ju's pregnancy. He seemed overprotective like that.

"Most will find lodging here in the city or return briefly to lovers and kin on other islands," Hakim assured me. "We are sure to lose a few to retirement, but I can't blame them. Between their portion of our commission fee and the prize money, they'll be set up nicely." He swallowed and set his cup on the saucer with a gentle clink. "A few might not wish to wait that long and will find berth on other ships, but we will have enough to sail when the time comes."

I nodded silently and regretted it when my head panged uncomfortably. As miraculous as healing spells and potions could be, one simply did not mess around with the brain. Madame Chén had said I was fortunate to be moving at all after the battering I'd given my skull, and that I was lucky headaches and a scar across my hairline were my only souvenirs.

Hakim's eyes widened, and he let out a surprised noise. "That reminds me, Cook sent you a package." He pulled a heavy-looking box from an unseen bag under the table and slid it across to me. "He said he risked his life to get it, so you better appreciate it."

I took it gratefully and weighed it in my hands. It was every bit as heavy as it looked. "Did he say what it was?"

"Not to me." He shrugged and then tilted the rest of his tea back into his mouth. He slid a hand into the pocket of his heavily embroidered silk vest and pulled out another letter. "There was also this. The man at the front desk asked me to bring it up."

It turned out to be a letter written on thick and expensive parchment. I didn't recognize the handwriting or the postmark, but I took it regardless.

"Thank you again, then." As I examined the letter more closely, Hakim finished his tea and stood up. "Do you need to head out?" I asked, biting back my disappointment.

He let out a soft laugh and rubbed his forehead. "Yes, you're not the only one I'm visiting today, and Captain Proulx wants me at our rooms by sunset." His smile grew wider and softer. "She wouldn't tell me why, but if it's what I'm thinking, I shall be a very happy man indeed."

I promptly decided I didn't want to know what he meant and dropped Cook's package on the table. Never ask about a couple's business unless they dragged you into it, as my mother liked to say. "Well, I won't keep you, then. Give my regards to the others. When I get out of here, I'll send you a message with where I'm staying."

Hakim thanked me and left with a promise to send someone up for my dishes. Waving once more, I slumped back into my seat and nibbled at a scone while considering my mail. The sigil on the seal revealed nothing—unless there was some hidden meaning in using Fortitude's crest for letters. I'd seen that symbol adorning the flags and guard uniforms around town. Hell, one of the merchants Cook and I visited my first time in Fortitude had sold tiny copies of the city flag for children to carry around.

But besides that, I'd only sent a few letters since we'd returned, and it was too soon to see any replies to those— and I didn't think my mother or my siblings would have access to such fancy paper unless something dramatic had changed while I'd been away. Not many people knew where I was staying right now, and most of those that did weren't aware of my role in our rather dramatic arrival.

Still, it did narrow down the list of potential senders dramatically. So dramatically in fact, that I had no idea who could've sent the letter.

Curiosity won out, and I pushed the package from Cook to the side and picked up the fancy letter.

It was heavy in my palms, and the ink was dark as night against the snow-white page.

To Edward Bardsley,

Alchemist of the privateer Vulturnus

Madame Chén has kept me abreast of your recovery and tells me you are well enough to leave your sickbed.

Please come to the keep at your earliest convenience. I wish to discuss details of your experiences in person. Bring this letter as proof for the guards, they will take you to me directly.

Kindest Regards,

Thaddeus the Black

Master of Fortitude

High Lord of the Dragons of the Flying Isles

I read the letter once. Then again. My eyes fell upon the envelope and the seal, and I nearly inhaled my scone.

The master of Fortitude had sent me a letter. Me. Personally. He wanted to meet with me.

I jolted to my feet, nearly overturning the tea set, and dove for the washroom. The master wanted to meet with me, and I'd barely combed my hair today. I rushed through my daily ablutions faster than was wise and nearly cut my own throat doing so. Fortunately, the damage was small and easily taken care of with a potion from the stock Madame Chén kept in each room.

My laces fought me as I rushed out the door, the master's letter stuffed in my pockets. I stopped briefly to tie them because the desire to not break my neck while I went down the stairs beat back the desire to win the battle against my footwear. The man at the front desk called a cheerful goodbye as I raced out the door, and I waved him off.

I wasn't certain what exactly the master wanted to question me about, but I wasn't going to keep him waiting any longer than necessary. Besides, he probably just wanted to ask me questions about the *Seabane*. Maybe the trackers the Liúwáng sent had finally caught up to them.

At least, that was the only reason I could think of that he'd ask me to see him. The only positive one at least. Shaking my head, I pushed that thought as far from my mind as I could. We were heroes. Even the Liúwáng couldn't hold my father's sins against me when I'd risked my life to save one of their clan heirs.

I slowed, my sense catching up to me as I did so. The master had called for me. Getting there would do me no good if I arrived looking like a drunkard fresh off a three-day binge. Smoothing down my shirt, I cataloged my appearance and had to admit I should've spent more time on it before I left.

I stopped in a small alley, one lit up by the early afternoon sun, and set about fixing what I could. My shirt was tucked in, my vest buttoned, and my boots retied so they didn't threaten to slide off with every step. A convenient window—with no one on the other side—served as a mirror to correct the sloppy way I'd tied my hair back. Combing it out with my fingers helped, but I wished desperately that I'd thought to visit a barber before today. My quick shave earlier was uneven at best and patchy at worst.

Still, I set my jaw and tied my hair back neatly. It wasn't perfect, but it wasn't like I could do much better. I could count the pieces of clothing I owned on one hand, and none were better than the rest.

Now that I was as put together as I could be, I set off again, my hand clenched tightly around the letter that was to be my ticket into the keep.

The streets here were emptier than the ones farther down in the valley, and I noticed more than one well-dressed individual turned their noses up as I passed. The stores were all higher-end, luxury goods that most people living nearer the harbor had no use for. They also, I noted gleefully, bore signs of damage along their upper levels. Almost like a ship or two had rammed into them at full speed. The only folks I saw dressed like me were the ones repairing that damage, and the fancy ones avoided the workers in the same way they avoided me.

Rolling my eyes, I picked up my pace. The keep wasn't far, and I didn't have time to worry about what random rich people thought about me.

On my actual approach to the keep, however, my confidence began to wane. When I handed the letter to the guard at the gate, she looked me over like a farmer looked over a horse at the market. She conferred with another guard, who agreed the letter looked legitimate, and the two called for a third guard to take me deeper in the keep.

If the outside of the keep was imposing, the inside was impossibly luxurious. Each hallway we passed through, each room I got a passing glance into only made me feel smaller, dirtier, and more insignificant. The ceilings loomed overhead as if to remind those walking through what kind of being owned these halls. The black stone floors gleamed so brightly, I could see my face in them. The paintings detailed what I assumed were historical events, each featuring a large black dragon missing a leg and wearing golden bands around his horns and remaining limbs. Alongside him was a dark-skinned human with gold beads decorating his hair, and unless I was wrong, that was real gold, not just paint.

In the end, the walk wasn't nearly as long as it felt. The guard brought me to a massive set of oak doors inlaid with gold dragons and jade ships. He stood alongside and gestured for me to go in.

I hesitated. In all my rush to get here, I hadn't really considered what that would mean. Beyond that door waited a dragon. The same dragon that hired the *Vulturnus*, and whose coin paid for each meal, potion, and good night's rest I'd enjoyed since we returned. He was as good as royalty in the Flying Isles, and as for me . . . I was an alchemist from a tiny village on a tiny island no one had ever heard of.

I must have hesitated too long, because the guard rolled his eyes, sighed, and grabbed my arm. Shoving the door open with one hand, he pushed me in with the other. The door clicked shut behind me, and I found myself in a cavernous room decorated with beautiful statuary and dozens upon dozens of plants in various stages of blooming. So many plants, I almost wondered if I'd been pushed into a greenhouse instead of a waiting room and that the guards were playing a horrible joke on me.

The only thing that held that thought back was that I wasn't alone. Two figures, a dark-skinned man in a wheeled chair and a person of indeterminable gender dressed in practical robes and a leather apron, sat on opposite sides of an ornate metal table in the middle of the room, surrounded by plush plant life and enough bookshelves to make the most learned mage faint in delight. Both turned to look at me while I took in the room.

"Don't just stand there, boy, come over here," called

the robed person, their accent giving them away as Chinese while they gestured for me to come closer. "It's rude to keep us waiting."

That was enough to break through my surprise. I started forward, first at a jog but slowing to a walk and then picking up again to something in between the two. "I beg your pardon," I said when I was close enough to speak without shouting, "but I received a letter. I'm Edward Bardsley, and I'm supposed to meet the master here. Are you two . . .?" I trailed off uncomfortably. The master wasn't here, but the man seemed familiar. Perhaps he was a descendant of the one who always appeared alongside the master in the paintings on the walls?

The Chinese person snorted. "I told you, he's too rural. Fan Ju said he couldn't even light his own lanterns."

The man raised a hand to silence the speaker. "Ke Xin, don't be rude. He's come a long way to speak with us." He turned to me and smiled.

The effect was incredibly disarming, like I'd come across an old friend unexpectedly or ran into someone singing an old favorite I hadn't heard in years. It was nostalgia made real, and I found myself smiling back as best I could, my anxiety melting away.

"That's better," the man said in a low voice. "I wasn't sure it would work, considering the situation." His chair rolled toward me with no evidence of anyone pushing it and stopped an arm's length away. He leaned forward, and the golden beads woven into his hair clicked against each other as he raised his hand toward me. "I'm Thaddeus, the master of Fortitude. It's a pleasure to meet you. Ke Xin's children have told me a lot about you."

My mouth worked open and closed, and I barely remembered to take his hand. "You're the master?" I asked in a squeaky voice. "But you're . . ."

"Human?" He wiggled his eyebrows and let out a thunderous laugh. "Only when I want to be."

"You're a shapeshifter," I breathed, hardly daring to believe it. "I mean, you're a shapeshifter, sire." My manners came late, but better than not at all. He'd been exceptionally kind to not comment on all the ways I'd been rude thus far.

All the same, it was hard to feel that any of that mattered at the moment. Now that I looked closer, I connected dots that had been in front of me the whole time. Just as the master as a dragon was missing a leg, so was the master as a man. The gold that lined his horns and his limbs became beads, earrings, and thick bracelets. The portraits in the halls on the way here weren't of a man and a monster, they were one person with two forms.

I felt like an idiot. Of course the master could turn into a human. None of the shops and few of the streets were large enough for him to inspect them personally like he was rumored to do annually.

"Please, call me Thaddeus," he insisted, patting my hand the way one would a child who'd just worked out the answer to a complex riddle. "Those who've done so much for my city deserve that pleasure at least."

I very much so did not want to do that. I wasn't sure I could. He was the master and I was a poor alchemist.

Ke Xin grunted and strode forward. "And I'm Ke Xin Shi, leader of the Shi Liúwáng in Fortitude and mother of two children that have somehow decided they like you. Now that we're all introduced, let's get down to business."

My breath caught in my chest, and I nearly swallowed my tongue. "You're Fan Ju and Min Li's mother?" I asked stupidly.

Of course she was. I only knew two Liúwáng siblings

who might be persuaded to call me friend and were also the heirs to a large Liúwáng clan. Not long after I was cleared for visitors, Fan Ju had sent me a note that said her mother wanted to thank me personally, but since I hadn't seen anything, I'd assumed she'd decided against it. I honestly hadn't expected to run into any member of their family until after the baby was born.

Ke Xin didn't answer beyond scoffing like I'd asked whether the sky was blue or if falling off the island would kill me. Instead she stomped off to the table and took her seat again, glaring impatiently at the master and myself.

The master chuckled and nodded to the table. "Come on, her family always gets annoyed when I waste time."

I followed the master back to the table and took the only open chair without prompting. Ke Xin kept glancing at me and frowning. Finally, she turned to the master and let loose in rapid-fire Mandarin.

The master answered in kind, never losing his pleasant smile or appearing anything but benevolent.

Ke Xin snorted. "Fine. If you're sure." She stood and stomped to a collection of potted trees.

The master didn't move, so neither did I, even as Ke Xin's grunts and complaints echoed back to us. When she finally emerged, she did so while dragging a large and exceedingly familiar chest with her.

That was the chest we'd stolen from the Van der Berg keep, my brain helpfully informed me. I hadn't seen it since before we'd crashed, but the hours I'd spent staring at it or working around it meant I knew it as intimately as I knew my own face.

Ke Xin and the master—Thaddeus, he said, I should call him Thaddeus—stared at me expectantly. I stared back. The metal chair dug into my rear, and I suddenly wished to be anywhere but here.

"Well, open it, boy," Ke Xin snapped, pushing me toward the chest. "We don't have all day."

Thaddeus took her by the arm and pulled her away from me. His chair creaked under the effort of pulling both of them back. "My friend, we expected this. He's not a mage; he barely has any power at all."

She snorted and tugged her arm free. "He is as skilled as one. Fan Ju said he kept the notice-me-not wards up even against the combined abilities of the Keats brothers."

"Yes, but that doesn't change his specialty. He's a potion maker, not a spell caster."

I wanted to protest the less than subtle derision of my abilities, but my words refused to slip past my teeth. Besides, he wasn't wrong. With my innate magical power being what it was—that is, almost nonexistent—I hadn't wasted time studying anything I couldn't use.

She snorted and rolled her eyes. "Fine, I'll do it, then."

My mouth gaped like a fish, and I didn't try to close it.

They must be incredibly close. That was the only reason I could think of why the master didn't try to stop her from opening the chest.

We had been under strict orders regarding that. We weren't to wonder what was inside or interfere with the seals or even glance at it sideways. We'd have forfeited our entire pay, sans expenses, if we did. The only reason it had been in my storeroom at all was because the captain wanted it in the most secure room on the ship in case it held some magical nonsense, and you couldn't beat an alchemist's workroom for that.

The hinges on the chest creaked as Ke Xin swung it open. I held my breath as she stepped out of the way, and I was treated to my first glimpse of the prize we'd nearly lost our lives for.

Pearls. Three of them, each bigger than both my fists

held together, and nestled in a decadent nest of red silk.

I stood for a better look without thinking about it. The others might as well have not existed.

The pearls gleamed in the light. It swirled around them, pulling it in and reflecting it out again in the most pure way I'd ever seen. It was like three stars had come down from the sky and found their homes here.

A melody hummed in the back of my mind. It was familiar to me, and I unconsciously hummed it back. No . . . not one melody. Three. A harmony with one part missing.

I stepped forward. The harmony sang sadly, a song of fear and loneliness and the desperate desire for safety. I knew this song. I'd been hearing it for weeks while I worked, slept, and ate. Unconsciously, I began humming again, but it wasn't quite right. The line I knew didn't fit anymore. I reached out, half expecting someone to stop me.

One moment, I'd been at the master's side, gazing unblinkingly at the pearls, and the next, I was seated on the floor and they were in my lap. The pearls were warm and pulsed like a heartbeat. The harmony in the back of my head sharpened and pulled, begging for me to add my voice to theirs, but I couldn't quite make out my line. I listened, fighting all the noise of the world and my own mind, reaching with my thoughts and my hands and my magic. I found my part in the harmony.

The pearls shone like a sun, blinding me to all else around me. Then there was a sharp crack, and the light vanished. I remained behind, on the floor by the chest, blinking up at the expectant faces of the master and Ke Xin.

The pearls had shattered, and in the ruins they left behind were three baby dragons with pearlescent scales.

Thaddeus let out a gentle gasp. He wheeled forward and reached out with one hand to run a finger along the largest hatchling's face. It let out a mewling grunt and pushed closer into his hands, digging its tiny claws into my leg and disrupting its siblings to do so.

"I knew it," he whispered, his voice thick with unshed tears. "They were waiting for you. They were late because they didn't want to come out without you."

Three presences pushed on my mind, a quiet hum I could barely hear over the background noise, but as insistent as hunger.

"What did I do?" I asked numbly, cupping the smallest of the three hatchlings in my palms. It laced its long and gangly body around my fingers and chirped at its siblings as if bragging about being held by me.

"They'll be hungry," Ke Xin said, sounding reluctantly impressed. "You'll need to feed them every few hours until they're old enough to decide their names and sexes. Their scales will change color about that time as well."

Thaddeus nodded and tore his eyes away from the babies. "Thank you. When Johannes Van der Berg stole my children, I thought I'd never see them again." He slid from his chair and collapsed next to me on the ground. The two larger hatchlings sniffed him, and the bravest ventured onto his lap.

"They're yours?" I asked stupidly before mentally hitting myself over the head. Of course they were his. He was the only adult dragon for miles around.

The hatchlings didn't seem to like me mentally berating myself. The smallest one hissed and bit—or more accurately nibbled—at my hand in punishment. The other two stumbled back to me, chattering up a storm and smearing the remnants of their eggs all over me.

"Yes," Thaddeus said reverently. "Mine and Shi's."

"Shi?" I glanced at Ke Xin out of the corner of my eye, and unfortunately, she saw.

"That's all the detail you'll get on that," she snapped, but somehow softer than before. "The only thing you need to know is that those dragons are considered family to my clan, and you are not, no matter how much they needed you to hatch."

That was fair. The Liúwáng kept their secrets close to their chest, and I was pushing things much further than I'd ever thought anyone could.

I looked back down and swallowed. All three hatchlings had curled up on my lap, and Thaddeus looked at them like they hung the stars in the sky. As I admired them, Ke Xin's words caught up to me.

"What do you mean, they needed me to hatch?"

"They bonded to you after your crew rescued them," Thaddeus said simply. "They felt your presence—the touch of your innate magic—when your crew broke into their prison, and decided you were safe. They refused to hatch until they knew you were here."

I hesitated before I spoke again, my feelings swirling around my stomach like a tide pool. "But . . . it wasn't my magic. It was Cook's. All I did was give it shape."

"You gave it will," Thaddeus corrected, raising his eyes from his children to glare at me. "There is no power on earth that will move on its own. It needs a guide to shape it, and a will to move it. Your will to keep your friends safe gave Cook's innate magic the power to do so. It was what made my children trust you."

Ke Xin came around to my other side and knelt on the ground. She picked up the remaining hatchling and cradled it in her palms. It chirped angrily at her before it settled down. "It's true," she said softly. "They knew you were a good person when you saved your friends, and when your captain put them in your workroom, they knew you would protect them too." Her voice dropped even lower when the hatchling curled into a ball. Gently, she deposited it back in my lap. "You heard their song, and they bonded to your magic. They've adopted you into their family, boy. Best not fight it."

***

It was dark when Thaddeus was persuaded to let me go, and even then, it was only to an opulent room deep within the keep. I'd tried to refuse, but he'd made it clear that no wasn't an option. He'd sent someone to gather my things, the few that they were, and they were waiting for me when I pushed the door open. My tiny bag seemed pitifully small next to the ornate bed big enough for my entire family to sleep without touching each other.

The hatchlings wasted no time in investigating my belongings.

I collapsed on the bed next to them and let loose a deep sigh. Thaddeus and Ke Xin had explained my role here succinctly. The hatchlings couldn't be far from me for a while. My innate magic, little as it was, was like a balm to them. If I separated from them for too long, they would go wild searching for me, and the stress might very well kill them.

Even if it weren't for my oaths as an alchemist, I knew I wouldn't have been able to refuse. Thaddeus would pay me well for my nursemaiding, but he made it clear I wasn't to leave Fortitude until his children could survive without me.

I didn't blame him.

One of the hatchlings let out a victorious squeak and fell out of my bag onto the bed. In its tiny mouth, it held a letter with Cook's familiar scrawl on it.

That was right. I sat up urgently and felt something

inside me unwind. Cook had given me something. I'd been so preoccupied with Thaddeus's . . . everything, I'd completely forgotten.

I gently took the letter from the hatchling, and it squawked in outrage. Angry chittering buzzed in the back of my mind, and I sent soothing hums toward it as I broke the seal on Cook's letter.

Lad,

I know you lost most of your things when the ship went down. I wrote to a mutual friend of ours, and they said they might be able to help.

They recommended this book. I tried to tell them that you weren't green behind the ears and knew your plants, but they insisted. They also said you're to open the big envelope after you meet with the master.

I didn't ask what they meant by that.

Cheers,

Cook

P.S. Kit says hello and to tell Alice we won't die if we go for a walk while she takes a nap. She doesn't listen to us.

I let out a huff of laughter, refolded the letter, and turned my attention to the package. It was large, entirely wrapped in brown paper and tied shut with twine, which two of the hatchlings had undone and were currently tugging back and forth between them.

Leaving them to the twine—and their sibling was more than eager to join them when it realized I wasn't doing anything interesting—I opened Cook's present.

Inside was a thick envelope and an alchemy textbook. More accurately, a botanical compendium. I'd had one like it before, but it hadn't survived the journey back to Fortitude. It surprised me how touched I was that Cook had gone to the trouble to get it for me even if he didn't know why I'd need it. A new one had actually been first on my list of things to replace once I had my pay.

I lost a few hours paging through it, showing the hatchlings different plants and potion guides whenever they showed interest and reading through the articles littered throughout the book whenever they looked bored. It wasn't until all three had fallen asleep over my legs that I remembered the other envelope.

This one was nearly an inch thick and bore no mark to indicate who'd sent it. I'd have tossed it aside if not for Cook's warnings and my own suspicions about the sender.

I was quite pleased to be proven right.

Boy, read the first line in a familiar blocky hand, *I've completely forgotten your name, despite the prodding of the master and your Cook, and I have little intention of learning it until you introduce yourself properly.*

If you listened to my warning, you opened this after you saw the master, and you now have three little ones hanging off you. Don't act shocked, the master consulted me first. It's not for nothing that I'm the greatest purveyor of interest on this half of Fortitude. There's little I haven't seen and littler still that the master thinks I can't discover.

Regardless of all that, you're trapped here. The master is aware of your position, and he does feel bad about it. He told me he wished to offer you the chance to improve yourself while you're stuck here, and he figured I may be able to point him in the right direction.

That brings me to the point of this letter. Delilah remains regretfully feline for the time being—the damned fool refuses all attempts to correct the situation—and I find myself in need of an assistant to run my shop and help in the lab.

I'll offer good pay for your time, and the little ones are more than welcome to hang around, provided they bother Konstantyn whenever he gets too annoying.

Attached you'll find a list of duties should you accept the position, and a labor contract. Return it to me signed or with proposed amendments by tomorrow morning.

Regards,
Mel
Alchemist, purveyor of interest, and tea maker

At the very bottom of the page, and stained heavily with tea, was a postscript.

By the way, I wouldn't worry about your crew so much. They'll be stuck here for a few months as well. A lot can change in that time, but I'd imagine your captain won't care if you find more stable employment for the time being.

The hatchlings each sent inquisitive hums toward me, shuffling as if on the verge of waking up, and I sent soothing hums back to them. They'd hear about it in the morning.

With trembling hands, I flipped the page and saw for myself just how certain Mel was of my acceptance.

On the second page, and the ten that followed it, was an application for employment with all the questions already filled out. Somehow—and I blamed Cook—Mel had gotten all my information correct, even my birthday and the names of the scholars I'd studied with back on St. Bernard. The list of duties was long, but not impossible, and they'd worked time into every day for my own studies and experiments.

All in all, it wasn't a bad contract. It was fair, even if some of the items were more unusual than I expected for a pawnshop, but whatever they meant by "minding the door to the elsewhen," I was sure it couldn't be worse than anything else I'd done. Besides, how many shops actually let the assistants experiment? Anywhere else would have had me paying out the nose for my reagents and lab space.

But it was the pay that had my eyes bugging out of their sockets. The only thing that kept me from yelling out in disbelief was the hatchlings sleeping around me.

Mel was offering enough to rent out a house in the

noble's district for a month each week. Additionally, they mentioned I was free to use their books, tools, and reagents as long as I cleaned up after myself. Between that, my pay from this commission, and Thaddeus's guilt money, my sister's tuition was nearly paid for.

My hands shook and my breath came short.

I'd done it. It hadn't taken a decade. It hadn't required me to sell my services to whatever merchant or backwater crew would take me. If I took this job, my mother wouldn't have to worry about me or my sister's schooling anymore. She'd know I was safe and we were taken care of.

It didn't take long to reach a decision. I nudged the hatchlings aside and scoured my room for a pen and ink. I signed before I could think better of it.

When I capped the pen and admired my name glistening on the parchment, it felt like a weight lifted from my shoulders.

I had work. I had a place to stay until the hatchlings grew. I had made friends and enemies and a few relationships that were somewhere in between.

Whatever happened, I had someplace to go and someone that would help me when I got there. This may have been the end of my first adventure, but somehow, I didn't think it would be the last.

Interlude 4

So ended my first voyage on the ship *Vulturnus* and my last outside of Fortitude for longer than I anticipated. The master kept finding new things to improve on the ship, and Captain Proulx was more than willing to allow someone else's coin to fund repairs.

The surviving crew came together often in the days that followed. We toasted to the ones we lost, and rejoiced in having survived at all. It was a bond that would follow us for the rest of our days. We might leave for new voyages and new berths, but at our core, we were sailors on the ship *Vulturnus*, and that was not a role easily cast aside in the battles to come.

But this wasn't our only adventure. In the days after I met with the master, Ke Xin insisted all surviving members of the crew needed to speak to a gathering of Liúwáng clans regarding what Johannes Van der Berg had done. The adventures that follow would fill another book entirely, so I will leave it there, but perhaps I will find time to put pen to paper once more and bring you another tale of my days sailing the flying islands.

ABOUT THE AUTHOR:

Ceril N Domace is an accountant, animal lover, and a dedicated dungeon master.

As a lover of fiction works great and small, Ceril has been reading age-inappropriate stories since her father failed to pull *The Silmarillion* from her grubby little fingers at age five. As a grown-up accountant, her spreadsheet compiling gives her plenty of time to make plans for a fantastic world that isn't plagued by balance sheets . . . and also has dragons.

On the rare occasions she manages to free herself from an ever-growing and complex web of TTRPG, Ceril enjoys taking walks and griping that all her hobbies are work in disguise.

www.ingramcontent.com/pod-product-compliance
Lightning Source LLC
Chambersburg PA
CBHW060153130626
46556CB00006B/2621